Smug Whistling Sands

Lou Elliott Mystery Adventure Series: Book 1

By

George Chedzoy

GEORGE
CHEDZOY

LOU ELLIOTT MYSTERY ADVENTURES:

To our son, daughter, nieces and nephews:

Thomas, Sophie, Charlotte, Sally, Ben, Beth and Albie

Smugglers at Whistling Sands
Lou Elliott Mystery Adventure Series Book 1
© George Chedzoy MMXI

First published by George Chedzoy, 2011 in eBook format
First edition in paperback, 2016
This book: First edition, first print

CONTENTS

CHAPTER ONE

Unexpected meeting

JACK stormed off towards the beach, shaking with rage. His younger brother was an idiot and he was not going to put up with one more minute of his company. How dare David talk to him like that! Who did he think he was, telling him to grow up and stop acting like a baby?

Jack thumped his fist into the palm of his hand, imagining it was David's smug face. Jack was 12 now – nearly a teenager – a whole year and a bit older than his brother. It was *David* who was the baby – the nerdy swot who always had his head in his books and trailed round after mum and dad.

Thanks to his brother causing a row, Jack had missed out on a huge English breakfast which mum always served up on holiday. David had deliberately finished off the tomato ketchup bottle, right down to the last dollop, leaving none for Jack – and then grinned at him. Jack, who loved ketchup, had gone mad at him only to be branded a baby not only by David but mum and dad, too. Jack had had enough of the lot of them so he stormed off, his food barely touched.

The fresh air was giving him quite an appetite. Blow David! Jack walked angrily and hungrily through the caravan site, across the main road, through the dunes and down onto the beach. His spirits began to lift as he looked about him. It was the first day of a two-week summer holiday at Abersoch on the Lleyn peninsula of North Wales. Jack was from a picturesque village called Malpas in Cheshire, a long way from the coast, so seaside holidays were a real treat.

The Welsh coastline stretched out into the far distance to his left. A handful of yachts cut gracefully through the water which sparkled in the sunshine as if sprinkled with a thousand diamonds. Straight ahead were two islands, St Tudwals East and West, surrounded by an expanse of blue. The eastern one looked large and sprawling, while the other was smaller and squatter, with a white lighthouse on the top. Jack longed to go sailing one day and land on those islands. They fascinated him.

Jack Johnson was a sturdy lad with short, mouse-brown hair, green eyes and a freckled face – and an even temper, most of the time. Now and then, however, he and David would fly at each other as they had that morning. David resembled him but was a slighter build, not so tall, and with fewer freckles. He was very studious and not exactly the outdoor-type. Their younger sister Emily was ten, good-natured, pretty, with golden hair and eyes as blue as cornflowers. She was a shy girl who rarely got cross and wisely keep out of the way when her brothers were arguing.

Jack ran through the soft sand down to the shore. It was good to be back. This had been a special place to him for as long as he could remember – and the Johnson family had been coming there since he was born. That said, he was beginning to feel a little restless, a touch fed up of going around with mum and dad, visiting the same old places. Nothing exciting or mysterious ever seemed to happen to him the way it did to children in books. Perhaps real life just wasn't like that.

The tide was nearly in and he had to jump onto nearby rocks to avoid a wave about to crash over his feet. He had explored here countless times and knew every fold and crevice, nook and cranny. He swiftly clambered out of danger.

Nestling amid the rocks were stone steps leading up the hillside to a steep path which disappeared around a bend.

A couple of times, Jack had climbed to the top of those steps but never gone any further. A sign hanging from a chain slung low across the path blocked the way. In big, bold letters, it said: PRIVATE, NO ENTRY.

Jack had never disobeyed a warning like that before but that day a bored, bad tempered voice inside him urged him to climb those steps and cross that chain. Suddenly, he bounded up them and, without even pausing for thought, hopped over into forbidden territory. He was now a trespasser! It was actually quite exciting.

He followed the path which veered away around another bend. It led him to a small, rickety wooden gate with paint peeling off. He cautiously walked up to it and peered into the smallish garden beyond. It belonged to a lime-washed cottage covered with red climbing roses. Its roof was tiled with dark slate, at one point rising into a peculiar, pointed turret. It was a charming, eccentric sort of place.

Jack was about to turn back when a stern female voice rang out from somewhere, making him jump: 'Didn't you see the sign – this is private property.'

Out of nowhere a girl appeared. She was probably not much older than him, yet he trembled under her gaze.

'Er, sorry, I just wanted to explore a bit . . .'

'You wanted to nose around and come snooping. I was watching you from the house, gawping into our garden. You'd better clear off before I get my parents,' she said, sharply.

'Ok, I'm going,' said Jack.

With that he promptly tripped over his own feet and fell sprawling to the ground. The girl sighed, opened the gate and reached down to him. 'Clumsy as well as nosy,' she said, reluctantly helping him up.

'Thanks,' said Jack, brushing himself down. 'Sorry to be a pain, I'm going now.'

'Well make sure you do – and don't let me catch you

spying again.' The girl's vivid green eyes fixed him in a final, withering stare from beneath a fringe of dark hair.

'I don't know why you have to be so rude. I was curious to know where the path led to, that's all. I don't normally come down to the beach on my own,' added Jack. Then he blushed, realising it was a silly thing to say.

'So you're a mummy's boy!' pounced the girl. 'I thought as much. Well you better get back, your parents will be missing you.'

Jack turned to go, then halted. What had she said? How dare she!

'I'm NOT a mummy's boy,' he retorted angrily, his face turning redder.

'Ooh sorry,' said the girl, a smirk crossing her face.

'It's my brother who's the mummy's boy,' Jack pointed out.

'Really, how old's he?' asked the girl, amusement getting the better of her annoyance.

'He's eleven and I'm twelve,' said Jack. 'And my sister is ten. So I'm the eldest.'

'You're the same age as me, although you look younger,' said the girl. 'Are you sure you're really twelve?'

'Right, I'm off,' said Jack, determined to get away before she had a chance to make any more cutting remarks. He felt very self-conscious about looking rather young for his age. He began to walk briskly away.

'Hey, come back,' she shouted after him. 'I didn't mean to offend you. You *do* look twelve. It's just that I look more like thirteen.'

Jack halted and turned round. That sounded more promising. 'You really think I look twelve, honestly?'

'Definitely. What's your name?'

'Jack Johnson.'

'I'm Louise Elliott, usually known as Lou,' she replied in a softer, more pleasant voice. 'Are you here on holiday?'

Jack nodded and hesitantly came a few steps closer. 'We got here yesterday evening, so today's our first proper day. Are you on holiday, too?'

'Yes,' said Lou. 'My parents own this cottage and we come here regularly. We arrived a couple of days ago.'

'It must be great having a place right by the sea with your own path to the beach,' said Jack. 'We've got a caravan on the site across the road.'

'It is great coming here,' said Lou, 'but lonely at times. I don't have any brothers or sisters to hang around with.'

'You must be spoilt by your parents if there's just you,' said Jack.

Lou laughed scornfully. 'They never bother with me. They are too busy. My dad is a freelance journalist who's always working, even on holiday. He doesn't have a spare moment. As for my mum, she doesn't care much for me at all. But I enjoy my own company – walking, sailing, fishing, climbing. I don't need other people around me.'

'My parents are nice. Boring, but nice, and they always want to do things with us, although nothing adventurous like sailing or anything,' said Jack.

Suddenly it occurred to him that his parents might be wondering where he had got to.

'Sorry once again for trespassing, I really didn't mean any harm. I'll get off now,' said Jack, turning to go.

'Oh, stop apologising, it doesn't matter. Listen, you could come sailing with me if you'd like. I could do with a crew. We could all go, me, you and your brother and sister.'

Lou's emerald eyes bored into his as if reaching into his mind. 'Well, do you not want to?'

Jack blushed again. They might be the same age but she was so much more self-assured. He felt shy and over-awed by this striking-looking girl with a sharp tongue.

'I don't think I want to,' he said, lamely.

'You *do* want to, I can tell. If you've got a mobile

phone, I could text you and we could arrange something. But I don't suppose your parents allow you one.'

That did it. Of *course* Jack had a mobile, now that he was nearly a teenager. He'd had it for Christmas from his mum and dad and was very proud of it. He pulled it from his pocket to show her.

'I don't need to look at it, just give me the number,' said Lou.

Jack did as she asked. She tapped it into her own mobile and stored it.

'Fine. Now leg it before my dad catches you hanging around,' ordered Lou, her stern voice returning. But she had a twinkle in her eye.

She vanished as suddenly as she had appeared. Jack stared after her, then swiftly headed off. He stumbled his way back down the path a little dazed.

Would Lou text him? Probably not. He told himself that he didn't care either way.

Back at the caravan, mum and dad were getting concerned.

'Where on earth has that boy got to?' dad Paul Johnson asked his wife Liz. 'Fancy clearing off like that just because David wound him up.'

'Perhaps he's been kidnapped,' suggested David. 'Hope so.'

The family's two dogs, Jenny, a golden retriever, and Barney, a border collie, had heard something. They pricked their ears up and woofed. The caravan door opened. Jack was back.

'Oh well, maybe next time,' said David.

'Next time what?' said Jack, walking in.

'Nothing,' said David. 'What have you been up to anyway? We've eaten your breakfast, by the way.'

'None of your business,' said Jack, ignoring the remark about breakfast.

But Jack couldn't keep a secret to himself for long. 'I went for a stroll on the beach. While I was on the rocks, I found a hidden path leading high up into the hillside. I followed it and at the end of it was a wild sort of girl with long, wavy dark hair and bright green eyes. She told me that she's got her own boat and has sailed all the way to the islands.'

'She's sailed to Ireland, wow!' exclaimed his sister Emily, mishearing.

'Erm Ireland, that's right,' fibbed Jack, getting carried away. 'And she's going to take me as well. She's going to arrange it.'

'Is she now,' laughed mum. 'Well, Jack, if you and she are going to sail to Ireland together, I think we better get to meet her first, don't you? Why don't you invite her round for tea sometime?'

'Yes go on, Jack, invite your imaginary friend round for tea,' hooted his brother.

'I will invite her,' retorted Jack, hurt they didn't believe him. 'She's keen to meet you both too, and take you boating,' he told his brother and sister.

'Oh I'm not getting in any boat,' said David, alarmed Jack's imaginary friend might be real after all. 'I'm far too sensible for that.'

'Really, David, it's about time you were more adventurous,' said mum. 'Jack, you can tell Lou she is welcome to come for tea anytime.'

'Right,' said Jack, 'I'll send her a text now.'

Only he couldn't, of course. She had his number, but he had not asked for hers.

'Er, I'll text her later I think,' he muttered, to gleeful laughter from his brother, now certain Jack was fibbing.

A few minutes later, his phone beeped. It was a text from Lou, saying sorry again for being abrupt and rude to him earlier, and asking if he wanted to meet that afternoon. Jack still felt somewhat bruised from their chance encounter but was intrigued by her and pleased she had got in touch. Also, he really had better ask her to come for tea, if only to shut David up. A minute later she texted him back to say she'd like to. Jack announced that she would be joining them – to looks of disbelief from his brother.

'Great,' said his dad. 'And bagsy I get her plateful if she does turn out to be imaginary.'

CHAPTER TWO

Lou comes to tea

AT 5pm came a knock on the caravan door. Lou was exactly on time. She never usually got to eat family meals round the dinner table, so this was an unexpected treat. Her parents had been fine about her going off by herself. They should have accompanied her or at least enquired where exactly she was going and what time she'd be back. But they didn't.

Jack opened the door and there, sure enough, was Lou. She grinned at him and said, 'ok, can I come in then?'

'This is Lou everyone,' said Jack.

'Hello Lou,' said Mr and Mrs Johnson.

No reply from David and Emily.

'David, Emily, say hello to Lou,' demanded their mother with a frown.

'Hello,' said Emily, eventually. David just grunted.

'Nice to meet you all,' said Lou.

'Nice to meet you, Lou, isn't it?' Mrs Johnson said, turning to David and Emily.

No response.

Lou shot a hesitant glance at Jack. This time, in unfamiliar surroundings, it was she who felt nervous.

'Sit down you pair,' said Mrs Johnson to Jack and Lou, 'and I'll get you a cup of tea. Do you take sugar, Lou?'

She shook her head. 'Just a drop of milk will be fine Mrs . . .'

'Johnson,' said Mrs Johnson with a smile, 'and this is my husband Paul. Now you'll have to excuse me, I need to get back to the kitchen. We'll leave you children to talk.'

Before long, the appetising aroma of roast chicken

filled the caravan. Mrs Johnson was a good cook who served up tasty, healthy meals. At Lou's home, it was different, where food came straight out of tins or the freezer. Tonight, for the first time in ages, she would have a plate of proper food in front of her. She was looking forward to it. The only trouble was, David and Emily didn't seem to want her there. She felt hurt and puzzled.

'Take no notice,' whispered Jack to her. 'They're jealous because they don't have any friends here themselves.'

'Well I'd like to be their friend, too,' replied Lou. Turning to Emily and David she said: 'You'll have to come and visit my den soon with Jack.'

'What den would that be?' inquired David, imperiously.

'My den in the woods,' she replied. 'It's inside a secret cave. No-one knows where it is or how to find it. I'd like you all to come. I can cook there, and do tea and coffee. I've got a little stove. You'd like it.'

'Have you got central heating, too?' asked David, sarcastically. 'I suppose that's where you keep your boat – the one you use to sail to Ireland in?'

'Ireland?' Lou, baffled, looked at Jack.

'Er, not Ireland, the islands, in the bay, Lou can sail all round them single-handed. She says we can go with her,' explained Jack.

'I keep my boat on the beach,' said Lou. 'My dad bought it me, it's got sails and a small engine.'

Jack turned to his brother and sister. 'Oh come on you pair, it would be fun. Lou could take us out in the boat. It would be exciting.'

'I'd like to go and see the den,' said Emily, 'but I'm not sure about going sailing. Anyway, mum and dad probably wouldn't let us.'

'Come to my den tomorrow,' said Lou, 'then we'll go to the beach and I'll show you my boat. You needn't sail if you don't want to.'

'Well I'm not going anywhere,' announced David. 'I've got a book I'm trying to read and I also want to do some more work on my Welsh. It's got rather rusty during term time.'

David, despite being only eleven, was something of a linguist. He was fascinated by languages and was teaching himself Welsh from a Teach Yourself book, much to the amusement of the others. He hoped, one day, to chat to local people in Welsh.

Traipsing through woods or getting drenched out at sea was hardly an appealing alternative. But he couldn't help feeling envious of the other two going off with this strange girl while he stayed indoors with mum and dad.

'Why don't you come too, David,' said Lou, as if reading his thoughts. 'You can read your books any time. Let's all go together.'

'No thank you,' he said, haughtily. 'It's not my idea of fun and anyway, I doubt mum and dad will let you.'

He was wrong. Mr and Mrs Johnson were intrigued by this adventurous twelve-year-old girl, and thought it a good idea for their stay-at-home children to become friends with her.

'She seems to have her head screwed on all right, that one,' said Mr Johnson to his wife as he helped her get the meal ready. She's got more spirit in her than the three of them put together, it will do them good to get a bit of fresh air and exercise.'

As for Jack, fresh air and exercise now seemed much more appealing. If the others didn't like Lou that was their problem. With her, their seaside holiday just might not be quite so boring after all.

CHAPTER THREE

The secret den

NEXT day, it was David's turn to be moody. He still didn't want to go with the others to Lou's den but nor did he want to stay behind.

'Why don't you go too, David,' suggested his mum, as she washed up the breakfast plates.

'Go on, David, clear off with the others, give your mother and me some peace,' added his dad.

'No, I have more important things to do, thank you,' he replied, obstinately. 'I'm going to learn how to use the Welsh perfect tense this morning. That's lesson five of my Teach Yourself book already.'

'Oh don't be so boring, come with us,' pleaded Emily. 'It will be fun.'

In the end they gave up trying to persuade him. Mrs Johnson gave Jack and Emily some sandwiches to take.

'You won't be too late, will you?' she asked. 'I'd like you back by three o'clock.'

'No problem,' said Jack. 'I've got my mobile with me so you can always phone or text.'

His mum smiled. Jack *always* had his precious mobile with him!

Jack and Emily had arranged to meet Lou on the rocks below the path to her cottage. They walked down to the beach together and Jack paused for a moment to gaze at the sea, the islands and the lighthouse.

'Come on dreamer,' said his sister. 'We said we'd be there for 11.30 and it's nearly that now.'

They clambered onto the rocks and Jack pointed out the steps leading to Lou's parents' cottage. He gazed upwards, waiting for her to appear.

'Boo,' came a voice right next to him. He span round and there was Lou on the rocks right behind him.

'I've been up since 6 o'clock, I've already been for a walk and gone sailing,' she said.

Emily eyed Lou suspiciously, as if there was something slightly out of the ordinary about her.

'Are you ready to come and see my woodland den?' asked Lou.

'There aren't any woods round here,' objected Emily.

'Yes there are,' replied Lou. 'You can't be very adventurous if you don't notice what is around you. There is a wood right by your caravan.' She led them back into their caravan site, passing near their own caravan and up the steep drive of a neighbouring one.

'Lou, what are you doing, we're trespassing,' whispered Jack.

'Don't worry, the owners aren't here,' she replied. 'Anyway, there is more than one way to the den.'

A wooden sign welcomed them to 'Ratty's Retreat', except they would not be welcome if the owners arrived and caught them, thought Jack, anxious that he was straying onto private property for the second time in two days. They followed Lou nervously to the garden at the rear which was skilfully carved out of the hillside.

It had originally been a mass of scrub and bramble, now it was crafted into an enchanting place with a proper lawn dotted with shrubs and flower beds, a small palm tree and huge rhododendron bushes. Garden benches looked out on the hillside below and blue lanterns hung from tree branches. The garden hummed with the buzzing of bees and the chatter of birds.

'Lovely isn't it?' said Lou, admiringly.

The garden bordered dense woodland which swept around the rear of the caravan park. Now Emily understood what Lou meant. The trees were easy to see from their very own caravan. But because she had never been there, somehow she had never really noticed them.

Lou and the others pushed their way through the bushes at the rear which seemed to close shut like swinging doors behind them. Jack and Emily looked around. They were about a hundred yards from their own caravan, but it seemed a long way away now that they were surrounded by trees.

It was still and silent, save for the swish swish of branches high above, whispering to each other. The woodland floor was a carpet of twigs, dead leaves and old tree stumps. It looked like nobody ever came here and in fact, nobody did, except young Lou.

Yet plenty of birds and small creatures made it their home. The owl Emily often heard hooting at night as she snuggled into her bunk was above somewhere, its head tucked beneath a wing.

Joe the crow was also fond of perching in the treetops and clacking noisily. He was one of Lou's bird friends and would have dropped down to say hello, but just then was on the beach playing chase with dogs on their morning walk.

Ahead was a path which Lou herself had made. It wound through the trees, then rose sharply and steeply to what looked like a solid mass of ferns, bracken and climbing plants forming a green curtain in front of them.

'You just have to push your way through, it won't hurt,' said Lou as the other two hesitated. 'It's got very overgrown. I need to cut it back a bit.'

They raised their hands as protection from the occasional thorn and stepped through the 'curtain'. Beyond was a small, grassy clearing and behind that a great wall of dark rock, jutting out of the hillside. A couple of feet from the ground, it opened out into a wide cave. This was Lou's den. It was also the most perfect hiding place.

'How on earth did you find this?' asked Jack.

Maddeningly, Lou just gave one of her grins. Her green

eyes sparkled with pleasure at the astonishment of her guests. It was the first time she had ever brought anyone to her secret den.

Inside was a small gas stove and kettle. 'Cup of tea, anyone?' asked Lou. 'I get my water from the stream we passed on our way here.' She lit the stove and set about making a cuppa. The three of them sat together on the smooth rock floor. Jack and Emily shared their sandwiches with Lou.

'I'm sorry there's not much of a view,' mumbled Lou with her mouth full. 'But it's rather nice here, just to escape from the world for a bit. I call this my woodland den. My other dens look out to sea – they're my favourites, to be honest.'

'What other dens?' asked Jack and Emily together. How many did she have?

'Three,' said Lou, reading their thoughts. 'I've got one at the end of the beach past the chalets, and another inside a cove at Whistling Sands beach.'

'Whistling Sands – that's miles away, you would have to drive there,' said Jack. 'We've been a couple of times with mum and dad.'

'Or sail,' pointed out Lou, 'or bike there. I don't have to wait for mum and dad to take me you know. And they wouldn't anyway. I have to keep myself amused, remember, they don't bother with me.'

'I can't believe it,' said Jack, sipping his tea. 'You're like some character out of a book. Three dens? We haven't even got one den!'

'That's ok,' replied Lou. 'You can share mine. We can have one each. Oh no, that would leave David out. Shame he wouldn't come today.'

'Oh he's too busy learning Welsh,' said Jack. 'He's such a swat and a bore at times.'

'*Chwarae teg iddo fo,*' said Lou in Welsh and not for the first time, Jack and Emily looked at her in astonishment. 'Fair play to him,' she said, translating into English.

'How come you can speak Welsh?' asked Jack.

'Oh, there's plenty you don't know about me,' replied Lou mischievously.

'Can you cook on that stove?' asked Emily, when she had finished her sandwiches. 'I would love to cook hot food outdoors.'

'Yes, but it's more fun on an open fire or a barbecue,' pointed out Lou. 'I'll take you out in my boat, if you like, we'll stow some food and my small cast-iron barbecue and have ourselves a feast. We could sail off round the coast and land at a beach that we'll have all to ourselves. I know a place where you get loads of driftwood washed up by the sea so if it's dry we can build a fire as well.'

Emily's blue eyes opened wide. 'That would be totally, amazingly brilliant,' she said, struggling to find the right words.

'See if you can get David to come too,' said Lou. 'He shouldn't be stuck in the caravan all day. It's so beautiful around here, he ought to be outdoors, enjoying it.

'You're quiet, Jack, are you ok?' added Lou, turning to him. 'You're coming aren't you?'

Jack was fine and was most definitely coming. He was busy daydreaming about their exciting plans. Sailing off in a boat round the coast to a secret beach, landing on the soft sand, gathering sticks for a fire and then cooking, all by themselves! What would his parents say to that?

'It would be like, I don't know, Robinson Crusoe,' he said, slowly.

Lou laughed. 'Yes, just like it. Only we'll be using matches, newspaper and firelighters to get the fire going and food bought from the shop in Abersoch.'

'Couldn't we make fire, rubbing two sticks together, like castaways in books?' suggested Emily.

'Don't be daft, this isn't a book, this is real,' retorted Lou. 'Why make life difficult? Anyway I've tried and it didn't work. So let's make sure that we remember the matches!'

The three of them chatted in the cave most of the afternoon. Lou showed them the paraffin lamp she used when it got dark, and her 'kitchen' area where she kept a couple of pans, tin plates and mugs and cutlery. Lou was old-fashioned in some ways, she preferred tin crockery to plastic, and paraffin lamps to battery-powered ones – 'more character', she told the others.

Suddenly there was a loud squawking. Joe the crow, bored with annoying the dogs on the beach had returned. He flew down to the cave entrance, opened his enormous black beak and croaked a tuneless song.

'Joe says hello,' said Lou. 'Sorry Joe, you're too late, we've eaten all the sandwiches.'

Jack's mobile phone beeped. It was a text message from their mum: '*where r u, u said u wd b home by 3. It's 10 past already. M*'

'We must go,' said Jack, getting to his feet, I had completely forgotten the time.'

'So, shall we go out in the boat tomorrow, and set sail for the mystery beach?' asked Lou.

'Oh we can't tomorrow,' replied Jack, pulling a face. 'We're supposed to be going with mum and dad shopping in Pwllheli and to Caernarfon to visit the castle. Would you like to come? They wouldn't mind at all.'

'No thank you,' replied Lou. 'It's nice of you but I hate trailing round shops amid crowds of people. What about Tuesday, the day after? I'll come to your caravan in the morning.'

'That would be great, Lou, I'd love that,' said Jack. Emily nodded, too.

Lou smiled at them, pleased that they were so keen on her idea. Suddenly it struck her that she wasn't on her own any more – she had found herself some friends and life might be a lot more fun from now on.

CHAPTER FOUR

David's strange encounter

IT was just as well they were not meeting Lou on Monday because it wasn't a nice day. It rained and rained. The weather forecast had been wrong too, which made it worse. It was supposed to be a pleasant summer's day, across most of the country at least, but the Lleyn peninsula was blanketed in dark, soggy clouds.

'I hardly think it's worth going out in this weather,' declared David after breakfast. 'I'm staying put.'

The boy was sitting at the kitchen table surrounded by his Welsh books. Emily was the other end of the caravan face down on one of the bunks, flicking through a girls' magazine. Jack paced up and down, irritably. He went to a window, pulled the net curtain back and looked out.

The Johnsons were lucky; they had one of the best-positioned caravans on the site. They could see the sea from the headland above Llanbedrog right round to the two islands. For years, towering fir trees got in the way but they were dying back, and the marvellous sea view was returning. But not that day. A mist hung over the coast and the sky was an obstinate grey. The rain drummed down noisily onto the metal roof and showed no sign of abating.

A seagull was perched on a nearby telegraph pole, its yellow beak resting on puffed-out feathers. Jack watched as it suddenly took off, soaring into the sky. It made him wonder what it would be like to have wings and fly up and up, far above the earth.

'Ok,' said their dad, putting his newspaper down. 'Are we going out or staying in?'

'In', said David. 'Out,' said Emily. 'Not bothered,' said

Jack dreamily, still staring out of the window.

'The weather is supposed to be improving later on,' said Mrs Johnson.

'What's it like for tomorrow,' asked Jack.

His mum laughed. 'Well, it should be fine and dry, but remember, that's what they said for today. It can often be different along the Lleyn peninsula.'

'Come on, let's go out,' said Mr Johnson, deciding a firm decision was needed.

'Nope,' said David. 'I'm staying put.

'You boring swot, David,' said Jack.

'*Cae dy geg!*' responded David in Welsh, 'shut your mouth!' he translated, triumphantly.

'David if you're learning Welsh just to be rude I shall take those books off you,' said his mum.

'Ok, how do you say "I'm a stupid little mummy's boy who never has any fun" in Welsh?' asked Jack.

'Right that's it, I'm off out,' said their dad, fed up with his sons. 'Anyone coming, or do I go by myself?'

In the end, all except David piled into the car and drove off, first to Pwllheli and then to Caernarfon. It did not turn out to be a bad day in the end, ambling around the shops and having a light lunch in a café. Somehow the damp just added to the charm of these very Welsh market towns.

Meanwhile, back at the caravan, David was angry and upset. He tried to convince himself he hadn't wanted to go with the others, although in his heart, he wasn't so sure.

Barney ambled up to him and sensed that he seemed a bit low. He gave his hand a warm lick. David stroked the dog for a while, then, to the animal's surprise, said impulsively: 'do you fancy a walk?'

Both dogs looked at each other and pricked up their ears, uncertain whether they had heard right. They had already had one walk and now David, of all people, was offering to take them for a second. David had surprised himself too – walking? In this weather? He didn't usually go outside even when it was sunny. The dogs leapt on him wagging their tails and barking. There was no changing his mind now. So off to the beach he went with them. With fresh sea air in his lungs he started to cheer up. This was actually a pleasant change from studying and swotting.

The sky and the sea were ash grey and unwelcoming, but it was breezy on the beach and the rain had eased. He glanced at the boats bobbing on their moorings, rocked from side to side by the waves. Few were under sail though, the sea was too choppy. David's complexion was pale but began to turn a healthy pink in the outside air. He laughed as he saw Barney bowled over by a wave crashing onto the shore. Barney loved water and often went swimming but Jenny was not so keen.

Before long David found himself opposite the entrance to the chalet park towards the far end of the beach. Llanbedrog Head loomed before him. He decided to walk right up to it. He had never done that before. That could be his little achievement for the day. He stared in fascination at the cliff face. Huge lumps of rock thrust out directly overhead, looking poised to fall.

Much of the cliff was a mottled gold and white with tufts of grass and a few shrubs protruding from crevices. The incoming tide was beginning to wash against an outcrop of the cliff but beyond that, the rocks retreated and there was more inviting soft sand. David took his shoes and socks off and paddled through the water to reach it.

At this point, the sheer rock face above gave way to what looked like a grass shelf half-way down, followed by a gentler slope to the shore. It would be pretty easy to climb up there, thought the boy. The view would be great.

With the dogs following, he clambered up, sometimes on all fours, to the shelf.

It was worth the scramble. He found himself on a narrow ledge which opened out to his right into a meadow of grass, buttercups, daisies and a host of brightly-coloured wild flowers. He could see for miles – right out into the bay and along the beach to Abersoch harbour.

A path led round a corner and David followed out of curiosity. Did anyone ever come here? It didn't look like it. In front of him, he saw what looked like the ruins of an old building, perhaps a look-out post, he wondered, or quarry workings. He didn't have much time to ponder the matter. Something on the ground caught the dogs' eye. They began sniffing at it. It was a cigarette butt with smoke still rising from it!

If David were still on the beach itself or in the dunes, he would have dismissed it as nothing more than litter, thoughtlessly discarded. But this plateau halfway up a cliff was well off the beaten track. He had expected to be entirely alone, especially in poor weather, yet clearly, he wasn't. There had to be someone else here.

Within a few seconds, he heard voices – men's voices – but could not place them. They were getting louder. They did not sound like tourists or casual walkers and he thought he detected a note of anger and urgency. David put the dogs on the lead and led them back round the corner. He tucked himself behind a bush climbing the rock face, pulling the dogs with him. He felt strangely uneasy and anxious not to be seen.

The voices got loud enough for him to make out actual words. He could guess that the men had come to a halt on the grass plateau where he had just walked. He couldn't resist peeping very cautiously round the bush. Sure enough, they were standing near the edge, looking out to sea.

At that point Barney stood up on his hind legs, whined

softly and gave a small woof.

'No, Barney,' David whispered, sternly. The dog sat reluctantly back down. The rain had started to fall softly again and Barney was getting restless. Jenny, who was more placid, just lay there, unconcerned.

Unwilling to move, David discreetly kept the men in view and began eavesdropping on their conversation. They clearly had no idea they were being overhead.

'Look,' said one of them, with a tattoo on his arm. 'They dropped the case on that island there.' He appeared to point towards St Tudwals East. 'They couldn't come ashore, there were folk on the beach having some sort of all-night party, so they dumped it on the island, under the wall in the far corner.'

The other man, sporting a gold earring, growled with annoyance. 'That's crazy. We should never have tried to deliver to this beach in the first place. There are always too many people about, day and night.'

He took out a map from his back pocket. 'Do I have to organise everything myself? For the next delivery, how about somewhere like this place, here.' He jabbed the map with his finger. 'If you ask me, that would be perfect – a quiet beach near Aberdaron on the north side, well away from campsites full of all-night party-goers. There won't be a soul about after sunset, and what's more, it's got a tarmacked road going right to it.'

'Fair enough, Griffo,' said the one with the tattoo. 'But what are we going to do about getting that case off the island?'

'That's something else for me to sort out, ain't it? Come on I'm fed up of standing here getting wet,' snapped the man with the earring, apparently known as Griffo. 'Let's go. I need a pint. We'll sort it out in the pub.'

The men walked to the edge of the shelf and were about to scramble down onto the beach. David gave a small sigh of relief. Then Barney, bored of being made to wait behind the bush, began to whine loudly.

'What on earth was that?' said Griffo. He turned round and stared hard towards the bush. David ducked quickly out of sight.

CHAPTER FIVE

Change of plan

THE boy froze. If the men caught him hiding behind the bush they would think he was spying! He shot Barney a furious look and hissed at him to be quiet. Mercifully, Barney took the hint.

Then came another strange, whining sound. This time the culprit was a seagull which had landed directly behind the men. The bird hopped towards them, opened its yellow beak and whined again, sounding admittedly more like a cat than a dog. Not to be outdone, a crow swooped and began a deafening clack clack, as if to say, 'go away, go away!'

'It's only the bloomin' birds,' said Griffo. 'Come on, Mick, let's get off to the Vaynol for that beer.'

The two scruffy, thick-set men with fat bellies and round arms headed down the slope and were gone. David waited a few minutes to be quite sure it was safe before getting slowly to his feet. In the far distance, he could see the pair walking off towards the village pub.

'Right,' he said to the dogs, 'let's go.' He led them back down to the beach.

David dug his fingers deep into his pockets. The weather was getting markedly worse. A raw wind was blowing the full length of the beach, whipping up the sand and spraying it into his face. The moored boats swung from side to side, their rigging clattering and jangling. The rain, stiffened with specks of sand, lashed David, soaking him from head to toe. His sodden jeans glued themselves to his legs like wet cardboard. This wasn't fun any more. He longed to get back.

He felt relieved to step inside the caravan. He was

shivering and not just from the cold and rain. David put the kettle on and changed his clothes while it boiled. It felt good to be dry and warm again. He got himself a cup of tea and a slice of home-made fruit cake and began to reflect on the strange conversation he had overheard. He pulled back the net curtains and looked out towards St Tudwals islands, still shrouded in mist.

It sounded like someone was hoping to deliver something to Abersoch beach late at night, but got spooked by the din from a party. So the item, whatever it was, got dumped on the islands instead. These people now wanted to switch their secret deliveries to a quieter beach where no-one would be about to see them.

David got the Ordnance Survey map of the Lleyn peninsula from the cupboard. He enjoyed looking at maps, even though he didn't much like going anywhere. Which beach did they mean? Whistling Sands, by the looks of it. It was the only one near Aberdaron on the north side, and it had a road leading to it.

But what were they bringing ashore that required such secrecy? Could they be smugglers? Yet weren't smugglers just characters in books, or from centuries ago? A tremor of excitement ran through him. Whatever would Jack and Emily think when he told them? He had a very interesting tale to share with them. He brightened at the thought and looked impatiently at his watch. He couldn't wait for them to return!

~~~~~

It wasn't so much that his brother and sister didn't believe him, they barely even listened. It was hugely disappointing. In they piled later that afternoon, mum, dad, Jack and Emily, with shopping bags full of food, drink and a couple of quaint vases his mum insisted on buying in Caernarfon. They were jabbering away about their exciting visit to Caernarfon Castle. 'It's a real castle' enthused Emily. 'In the olden days they used to lock up baddies in the dungeons – thieves and smugglers and . . .'

'I saw some smugglers today, on the beach, they were plotting, they are bringing in a delivery, they are going to come in the middle of the night . . .' spluttered David.

It was worth a try, but by now David was back behind the kitchen table, his Welsh grammar books spread out in front of him. It didn't look convincing. Surely the only smugglers he would have met that day were in a Welsh translation exercise.

'So what have you really done with yourself while we've been out, David?' asked his father, glancing at all the books. 'How's the perfect tense coming along?'

'Actually,' David began but gave up. There was no point. To them he was just boring David, head in his books, learning a funny language.

As for Jack, his thoughts were on one thing only – the following day with Lou. Sailing round the coast to a far-off beach, making a fire and lighting a barbecue! He could hardly wait!

~~~~~

The following morning came a knock at the caravan door. A split second later, it was opened by Jack.

'Come on in Lou,' called Mrs Johnson. 'There's tea in the pot if you fancy a cuppa.'

Parents who made you tea in the morning! Amazing!

'Hello everyone,' she said, stepping inside. 'Who's sailing then?'

'All except David at a guess,' said Mrs Johnson.

'David, why don't you come too, we'll have a great laugh,' said Lou.

'No thanks, I'll be fine here. I had some fresh air yes-terday, and I've got rather a lot of work to do on both

Welsh grammar and vocabulary,' he announced with a lofty, dismissive air. David still felt cross that no-one had been interested in his little adventure the previous day.

Lou's emerald eyes locked onto his. 'I would really like you to come,' she said in that soft, hypnotic voice of hers which was almost impossible to refuse. The girl had a strangely powerful effect on people, even David.

'Where are you going, anyway?' he asked, hesitantly.

'We will sail my boat from Abersoch to the end of the peninsula, past Aberdaron and round the other side to Whistling Sands,' said Lou. 'I thought we could even camp for the night if your mum and dad will let you. I've planned our voyage and I've already packed a few things. We could just do with some food rations if that's ok, Mrs Johnson. Have you got anything we could barbecue?'

'Of course, that's no problem,' said Mrs Johnson. 'I'll find you a few things. We don't mind them spending a night camping, do we Paul?' she added, turning to her husband.

'No not all, it will do them good,' he replied.

'Whistling Sands – that's the beach near Aberdaron isn't it?' asked David.

'That's right, it's the closest one to Aberdaron on the north side of the peninsula,' said his dad. 'I'm pleased to hear you taking an interest, David.'

The boy fidgeted slightly and looked alarmed. Lou planned to take Jack and Emily to the very beach he suspected the smugglers of using!

'In that case, I er, I'm not sure you should go,' he said, hesitantly. 'It could be dangerous.'

'What is he on about now,' said Jack. 'Is he talking in Welsh again?'

'No I'm serious. I think, I've reason to believe, there are bad people using that beach. People who may come in the middle of the night,' said David. 'We don't want to get into any trouble.'

'We, who is we?' asked Jack. 'I didn't think you were coming.'

'I'm not but I don't think you lot should go either,' replied David.

'Are you for real?' exploded Jack. 'Mum, dad, will you tell him to shut up. He's too much of a baby to come with us and have any fun but he doesn't want us to have any either.'

'What exactly are you talking about, David?' asked their dad, looking exasperated.

So David explained, or tried to. He told them about his walk on the beach the previous day and how he overheard a conversation between two strange men called Griffo and Mick discussing a case dumped on St Tudwal's islands, and plans for another delivery to a beach near Aberdaron which he guessed was Whistling Sands.

'I don't know what it is but they are bringing in something secret that they don't want anybody to know about,' added David.

'Oh what a load of rubbish,' said Jack, fuming with rage. 'It's funny you didn't mention this before. How come you didn't tell anyone yesterday when we got back?'

'I tried to, but you wouldn't listen,' said David, falteringly. 'You were too full of your own stories about Caernarfon castle and dungeons and so on. You weren't interested in what I had to say.'

'You didn't try very hard to get us to listen, did you? And now you're trying to scare us off because you don't like Lou and you don't want us to be friends with her,' shouted Jack. 'You can't bear the thought of us going off and having a good time, even though you have no wish to come. You're pathetic.'

'I'm telling the truth!' whimpered his younger brother, tears in his eyes.

'I'm ashamed of you at times, David,' chipped in his

father. 'You're making a fool of yourself.'

Jack's face lit up. He glanced at Lou whose cat-like eyes were fixed on David. A highly perceptive youngster, she could usually tell when people were making things up.

'I believe him,' she said, quietly.

Jack opened his mouth to say something but no words came out.

'Don't get upset, David,' she commanded. 'I know you're telling the truth, you are trying to warn us of danger and that's the right thing to do.'

'I don't think I want to go now,' said Emily. 'I'm a bit scared.'

Somehow, the fact that Lou believed David changed everything.

Lou gave his shoulder a rub. 'Well done for telling us. It shows that you care.' She turned to the others. 'It's ok. It's not a problem. We can do something different. I for one don't want to camp on a beach used by smugglers in the middle of the night. At least, not without being prepared.'

'I just don't believe it,' said Jack, looking like he was about to burst into tears.

'You boys are such babies at times,' scolded Lou scornfully. 'Why don't we go for a sail round the bay here, instead? We can take our barbecue and land on the islands and have a nice afternoon together. We can also take a look for the case the smugglers may have dropped off. As for you David – you're coming, ok?' she said, turning to him. It was more of an instruction than a question.

'Ok,' he replied, to his parents' astonishment.

On reflection, their change of plan didn't strike Jack as such a bad alternative after all. It would be fun sailing off to the islands and landing on one of them. They had never, ever done any such thing before. And he relished the thought of scouting around for the smugglers' case –

they would either find it, which would be very exciting, or they would find out that David was fibbing – which would be even better!

CHAPTER SIX

Off to the islands

L OU dragged the launching trolley up the sand, waded into the water and jumped into the boat.

'All aboard,' she cried. She rigged up the sail, took hold of the tiller and they were off!

Lou and her new crew didn't make directly for the islands but pottered around the bay for a bit. The weather was totally different from the previous day. The sea was once again a rich, glittering blue and the angry wind which had hurled sand and rain at poor David now gently ruffled his tousled hair.

Lou loved playing skipper. A natural leader, she bossed her new friends about, telling them which ropes to hold, and how to duck when the boom swung over.

'When we sail into the wind, we need to tack,' she instructed. 'Each time we change direction, the skipper shouts 'ready about', then pushes the tiller right over.'

Within half an hour, all of them, even David, had taken turns at the tiller and were starting to feel like sailors. David was enjoying himself as much as anyone although he winced a couple of times when extra-large waves hit the sides and spattered spray across his bare knees.

Lou swung the boat out towards the islands. As they approached, the white lighthouse which looked so far away from the shore appeared much bigger – so too did the islands themselves. David's heart sank a little. Trying to find a hidden case on St Tudwals East would be no easy task. Something else troubled him: the smugglers' muttered reference to 'under the wall, in the far corner'. What did they mean? David stared hard at the eastern island. There was no wall, let alone a corner! The words went round and round his head, but didn't seem to make sense.

The boat was getting closer now and the children, as if in a trance, gazed at the lighthouse on the western island. It looked a pretty building, gleaming brilliantly white in the sunshine. It stood proudly inside its own grounds, as though it had its own garden.

'I'm not sure where I can land, you know,' said Lou, as they approached Tudwals East. 'I'm surprised your smugglers chose the East island – the other one has got a proper little jetty.'

Suddenly a thought struck David. How did he know for sure the smugglers meant the eastern island? They looked like they were pointing to it, but from where he crouched they might have been pointing to the other one with the lighthouse – *surrounded by a low wall!*

'Erm, sorry but I think it could be St Tudwals West,' he announced.

Jack rolled his eyes skyward. 'This fairy story just gets better,' he crowed.

'Suits me, much easier to land there,' said Lou. 'I've always fancied a look round this lighthouse.'

'There won't be anyone in will there?' asked Emily.

'No,' said Lou. 'They don't man lighthouses these days. They used to have a lighthouse keeper stationed there though. You can see the keeper's dwelling alongside it.'

'Why don't they still man them?' Emily asked.

'Would you want to live offshore in a lighthouse all year around, cut off from the mainland?' replied Lou. 'There hasn't been anyone resident on St Tudwals West since the 1920s. That was when they put in a special gas-powered lamp which would automatically come on at night and switch itself off during daylight. Then in the mid-1990s it was converted to solar power, so during the day, the sun's energy provides the electricity needed to light the lamp at night.'

'Look over there!' cried Jack, interrupting the history lesson. 'I'm sure I saw a seal!'

'Yes! I saw it too,' said David, feeling glad he had come by now.

'Grey seals are quite common round here,' said Lou. 'Sometimes you even get porpoises and dolphins.'

'How do you know all this?' Emily asked Lou, admiringly. 'You seem very clever.'

Lou smiled. 'An old chap called Eifion, whom I see walking along the beach sometimes, tells me all kinds of things. He's lived here all his life and knows everything there is to know about the Lleyn peninsula. I practise my Welsh on him, too. I'll have to introduce you, David.'

David wasn't thinking about Welsh just then. He was excited about that case. Surely that's what they meant – it was in the grounds of the lighthouse – under the boundary wall in the far corner.

Lou collapsed the sail as they approached the jetty. 'Take an oar, Jack,' she told him.

The pair of them rowed alongside the jetty and Lou grabbed the rusty iron ring embedded into the concrete. She looped the rope through and deftly tied up.

'Welcome to Smugglers' Island!' she said, grinning, stepping ashore.

The children clambered out, heaving their heavy rucksack with them and a large rug to sit on. They could scarcely believe that they had just set foot onto a tiny island surrounded on all sides by the sea!

'I am starving,' said Lou. 'Let's have some food before we do anything.'

Save for the lighthouse in the middle, most of the island was rather featureless. It was covered with scrubby grass without as much as a tree, shrub, gorse bush or clump of heather in sight. Its steep slopes fell away sharply to seaweed-strewn rocks all the way round. It didn't have its own beach or anything. But it didn't matter. The children were simply delighted to be there. They had an island all to themselves! That's what made it so magical – it was their own little kingdom.

They laid out the rug in the centre, just beneath the northern section of wall running in a rectangle around the lighthouse. It was a good, flat stretch of grass with an excellent view towards the mainland and more sheltered than if they'd sat the other side, facing the open sea.

Lou had packed a portable barbecue which she open up and then lit. The aroma of charcoal smoke and grilled food soon rose into the air. The coast of the Lleyn peninsula stretched out into the distance. The beach near their caravan site ran like a strip of gold along its edge, shimmering in the summer heat. There were loads of boats too, yachts large and small and speed boats zipping from one side of the bay to the other. Sound travels easily over water and yells and laughter could be heard from sunbathers.

Emily glanced the other way at the lighthouse looming above them. It really did look so much taller and grander than from the shore.

'I feel like it's watching over us,' she said, and the thought made her shiver slightly.

David had been itching to search for the case but for now was happy to laze on the rug and bask in the sunshine. Jack and Emily were too. Lou had brought her book and was soon face down on the rug engrossed in it.

'Another drink anyone?' asked Jack.

'Yes please,' said Lou, stretching and yawning. 'You know I could lie here all day but I suppose we better get up and look for that case, once we've had another cuppa. You sure you're not making this up, David?'

He scowled and told them what he remembered about the wall and the far corner.

'Ok, but there might be some sort of wall on the other

island, you know,' said Lou, yawning again. 'There is the remains of a monastery, I believe, but you're right, this is the more likely of the two.'

The children got up and strolled to the gate leading into the lighthouse grounds. They opened it and looked along the walls.

'The far corner will be the one furthest from the lighthouse I should think,' said Jack.

In one corner stood a hut with what looked like a mini windmill on top. Lou pointed out that it was actually a wind turbine to generate electricity. The children went over to the hut but could see nothing through its opaque windows.

'Perhaps the case is locked inside,' said David, disappointed.

'Not necessarily, smugglers wouldn't have a key to the place, would they?' said Jack.

'Let's try the other corner.'

They walked along the walls keeping their eyes glued to the ground. At the other end were small rocks, stones and clumps of soil piled against the wall.

'Nothing,' decided David.

'You give up too easily,' said Lou. 'Take a look under the stones. It looks to me like the ground might recently have been disturbed.'

David crouched down and began slowly moving the rocks and stones. Jack went to help but Lou stopped him. 'Let David do it,' she whispered.

There *was* something underneath the rubble, wrapped in polythene sheeting and embedded in the soil. He felt his way along the side and touched some sort of handle. He could just about grip it through the protective wrapping. He gave it a really good tug and out it came! It was a fairly easy task to pull away the polythene. Underneath was a dark, rectangular, leather-bound object. David stood up and held it under the bright sunlight for them all to see.

It was a briefcase, a perfectly ordinary briefcase, the sort you see businessmen walking about with all the time, although this had streaks of mud over it if you looked closely. Yet why was it there, buried in the grounds of an offshore lighthouse?

'Wow!' said Jack, open-mouthed. 'Looks like David wasn't fibbing after all! It must be the case, the one the smugglers were talking about! Mustn't it, Lou?'

'Yes, it must be. And it's locked, there's no way of opening it. We'll have to take it back with us,' she said.

'Oh,' said Emily. 'Should we do that because it doesn't belong to us?'

'No Emily, it doesn't. But if this case was put here by smugglers, it's only right we take it and find out what it contains – and whatever it is won't belong to them either,' reasoned Lou. 'Well done, David!' Lou turned to him and gave his arm a squeeze. 'You've done brilliantly and proved you were telling the truth. Are you glad you've come now?'

David blushed with pride. Today hadn't turned out so badly after all. In fact, this was even more fun than learning Welsh.

'Very glad, and I really don't want to go back, this is great,' he said. 'Can we stay a while longer Lou. It's so much fun here.'

'I don't see why not,' she said.

Then she hesitated. Lou had a feeling something wasn't right. She had a rare ability to sense danger. The girl looked about her. She stared out to sea. Boats everywhere, just as before.

'I don't know,' said Lou, distantly. 'Perhaps we have been here long enough.' A flash of sunlight caught her eye from a motorboat some distance away. 'I wonder what that boat is doing, over there.' She pointed. 'It's not moving, it must be anchored.'

'It's probably full of lazy people enjoying a picnic like

us,' said Emily.

'Hmmm. What a shame I don't think I brought my binoculars,' said Lou. She checked the pockets of the rucksack but she was right – she hadn't. 'You know, I really think it's time we got back.'

'Oh but it's a lovely day and we're not in any hurry,' said Jack.

He was right, the sun still shone, it was only mid-afternoon and it seemed a shame not to make the most of the good weather.

'It might be pouring again tomorrow,' added Jack. 'And look, there are still a couple of kebabs and chicken drumsticks left. Have we got any more charcoal?'

'Yes, in the bottom pocket of the rucksack,' said Lou absentmindedly, staring at the motorboat.

'Great,' said Jack, I'll soon get the barbecue going again.

'No!' decided Lou, suddenly and decisively. 'I said we should go. We're having a lovely day but we have just discovered something strange and I have a funny feeling we are being watched. We have something important in our care. We should get it to shore as soon as we can.'

Emily shivered and looked around her. Suddenly every boat she saw seemed to spell danger.

'Don't worry, Emily,' said Lou with a smile. 'It's probably my imagination. Just humour me though will you. Let's go.'

The others felt disappointed but they did as Lou said, cleared up, packed the rucksack and loaded the boat. Lou got the sail up and pointed the tiller towards the beach. She glanced out to sea to reassure herself the motorboat was still anchored. Her sharp green eyes spotted white foam under its bows. It was moving.

'Take the tiller Jack, head directly for our bit of the beach. Let the sail out a little,' the girl commanded.

Lou felt for the petrol can under her seat, grabbed it and

filled the tank of the boat's outboard engine. She took the starting rope and yanked it. The engine spluttered. She pulled again and it roared into life. The boat leapt forward, powered now by motor and sail.

'I am worried about that boat behind us,' she said to the others. 'It's started to move in our direction, I want us to get back as soon as we can.'

The others followed her gaze. The boat was coming their way and appeared to be gaining speed.

'Don't worry,' said Jack to David and Emily, sensing they were alarmed. 'They are probably holidaymakers like us but Lou doesn't want to take any chances.'

The wind got up and Lou let out the sail further. She steered as close into the wind as she could for maximum speed. The motorboat was getting steadily closer, but the gusting wind had given them a good extra push. There were two men in the boat, both with dishevelled dark hair. Could they be the same men whom he saw the previous day? And was that the glint of a gold earring catching the sun?

At last, they reached shallow water.

'Jack, jump out now and get the launch trolley, bring it into the sea and I will steer the boat on top,' instructed Lou. 'We'll drag the boat onto the sand and as soon as we do, we must run as fast as we can back to the caravan site.'

Jack leapt out and got the trolley. Lou deftly guided the boat on, jumped out and helped him pull the boat onto dry land. David handed Jack the heavy rucksack, then he and Emily clambered out. David held the briefcase tightly in his arms, determined not to let it go.

'Give me the case,' said Lou. 'Let me go in front of you. Come on everyone!'

The children tore past sunbathers and hurtled through games of beachball and cricket, as fast as the soft sand would let them. Jack glanced over his shoulder. The men were ashore too, and running up the beach.

'They're after us!' he cried.

The children raced through the dunes, then along the path to the busy main road. They were in luck! There was nothing coming. They scampered across. The entrance to the caravan site was just a few yards away. But they weren't safe. The men had reached the road and were about to cross. Luckily, a convoy of five cars came round the corner forcing them to wait.

'Come on!' cried Lou.

The children ran into the site, past the security barrier and along the road to where it forked. But they were getting out of breath and their caravan was up a steep hill. There was no way they could out-run two burly men. They looked at one another in despair. They were certain to be caught!

CHAPTER SEVEN

Lucky escape

'STOP,' said Lou, panting. 'Jack, take the rucksack off your shoulders and hold it in front of you with the rug over it. Make it look like you're hiding something. Make them think you've got the case.'

He nodded. With that, Lou was gone, swift and nimble as a cat, diving off the road with the mysterious case and losing herself amid the endless rows of caravans. She was much fitter than the others and quickly got her breath back. She zigzagged left, then right, then left again. She paused for a minute and looked behind her. If no-one followed she might just have time to sprint through the site and into the adjacent field. It was another way to her woodland den. But it was vital that she was not spotted. She could not risk being tracked back there, of all places.

To her horror, she caught a glimpse between the caravans of a smuggler steaming along a neighbouring row! She tore off again, heading downwards through the site. Each row of caravans and chalets was separated by grass lanes, most of which were dead ends. There was no way she could now attempt to get to her den via the field. She had to hide, and fast.

Lou looked desperately about her. A caravan a short distance ahead was bordered by a trellis fence, with a huge hydrangea bush growing over the towing bar. No car was parked outside it. With any luck that meant no-one was staying there. She slipped through its gate and hurled herself under the caravan, pulling the case with her and sinking deep into the bush out of sight.

She was trembling and her heart was beating. Were those men the same ones that David had seen talking on the beach the day before? Either that or they were members of the same gang. They must have been watching the island and spying on them, through a telescope or powerful binoculars. That would explain the flash of sunlight from their boat. They probably saw David dig up the case and observed them sailing off soon afterwards. They had got away just in time.

Lou would have to stay put until the danger was past. She wriggled into a better position so she could see. She felt a little calmer now and her breath was coming easier. She hoped the others were ok. To her dismay, she heard footsteps above and floorboards creaking. There *were* people in the caravan she was hiding under! Thank goodness they hadn't seen her dive beneath it. They were coming out! In front of her appeared a pair of wrinkly legs stepping onto the patio.

'I enjoyed that nap, let's get some fresh air, dear, shall we, while it's still nice,' came the voice of an old lady. 'Bring the teapot will you and I'll take the scones. Oh and there's some jam in the cupboard. You like a little jam on your scones, don't you?'

'I do, my dear, I do like a little jam on my scones,' an elderly man chuckled in reply, 'in fact I like a lot of jam on my scones.'

Lou groaned. Now she would be stuck until this quaint old couple had finished afternoon tea, and that might take some time. Then, she caught sight of something far worse. 'Oh no,' she said, under her breath. The smugglers! They were walking between the rows of caravans looking under every one.

They were searching for her and the case! She couldn't crawl out the other side either, a chicken wire fence blocked her way. She was trapped, there was no escape this time. She dug herself deeper into the hydrangea but they would have to be blind not to spot her.

The elderly couple noticed the men too and eyed them

curiously. 'Eric, what do you think those men are up to, looking under everyone's 'vans? They seem a strange pair if you ask me. One of them appears to have a tattoo on his arm and the other one – goodness me – is wearing an earring! And neither can have shaved for days.' The old woman screwed up her nose in disdain. 'I've never seen them on this site before, have you?'

'I'm not really sure, dear, I don't know half the people on the site these days,' said the old man.

His wife took another sip of tea and carried on watching. As they approached, she called to them. 'Excuse me, may I ask what exactly you're doing? Have you lost something?'

'We're er, looking for our dog. It's gone missin'. We think it might be hiding under a caravan,' said the man with an earring in a rough-sounding voice.

'Well why don't you call for it then?' replied the old lady.

'Erm, good idea,' said the man with a tattoo.

'It's a bit shy,' said the one with an earring, at the same time.

'What breed is it?' asked the old lady.

'Retriever,' said the one with the earring.

'Labrador,' said his mate, a split second later.

'Erm, it's a sort of retriever, labrador cross,' explained earring-man, who seemed the brainier of the two.

'I see,' replied the woman, disbelievingly. 'Well let's hope you find it.'

He scratched his fingers across his rough chin. 'Er, would you mind if we took a quick look under your caravan, madam,' he asked, rather too politely.

'Yes I'm afraid I would mind,' said the old lady sternly. 'I don't want strangers nosing around my property. I'll take a look for you myself. What's its name?'

'Rover,' said earring-man quickly, before his tattooed pal had a chance to open his mouth.

The old lady slowly bent down. 'Rover, are you there, Rover?'

A vivid pair of green eyes like those of a cat rather than a dog stared back at her through a fringe of dark hair, making her recoil in fright.

'Shhhhh,' hissed Lou. 'Don't say a word.'

Somewhat shaken, the old lady straightened up. 'No, I'm afraid Rover isn't under my caravan,' she said, quite truthfully. 'But there is a little mouse. I think I need to sit down, it gave me quite a shock.'

The men scowled at her and moved on to the next caravan. A little mouse indeed!

'Daft old bat,' muttered tattoo-man.

When they were a good distance away, the old lady crouched again and called to Lou, 'it's ok dear, it's safe to come out now. They've gone. You poor thing. Were those men after you? Whatever for? I knew they weren't looking for a pet dog.'

Lou scrambled up, clutching the case, her eyes darting wildly.

'You look like a cornered animal. Come inside the caravan. I think there's still some tea in the pot.'

'They are bad people,' said Lou, 'they wanted to take my case.'

'Well they won't get it, dear, we won't let them, will we Eric?'

Eric shook his head. 'No, Edith, we certainly won't.'

The old lady poured Lou a cup of tea and a jam scone, which she took gratefully.

'Aren't there some strange people about? In our day, we didn't even need to lock the front door. I never thought we would see criminals turn up here at Abersoch of all places.' She eyed Lou's briefcase. 'I say, that's a serious-looking case for a young lady to be walking round with on holiday,' she remarked, curiously. 'There's mud all over it too, did you fall over?'

'Yes,' said Lou, 'while trying to get away from those men. I keep my school stuff in it, I've got some holiday work to do.'

It was a fib but she had to say something. The old lady was becoming a little too nosy. Lou ached to get back to the safety of her den but she mustn't rush to leave, in case those men were still about.

'This is lovely tea, you're very kind. I don't suppose there's another cup in that pot is there?' she asked

The couple beamed at her. How nice that this pretty young child should wish to stay chatting to them! There weren't many youngsters like that.

'Oh, I should think it's a bit stewed by now but if you're in no hurry, we'll brew up another pot,' replied the old lady. 'Put the kettle on again, Eric.'

So Lou stayed where she was, making small talk and sipping tea. She liked them both, they reminded her of her own grandparents whom she hardly ever saw, but she yearned for her den and was worried, too, about the others.

Half an hour passed and Lou, with a quick glance through the windows, decided it was safe to go. She thanked the couple for their hospitality and promised to drop by again.

'Goodbye my dear, it was lovely to meet you,' said the old lady. 'You can hide under our caravan anytime!'

Lou grinned and gave them a wave. Then, with the case under her arm, she swiftly headed towards the bottom of the site, past the disused shower block, over the wooden gate and into the field nearby. She plunged into the long grass and crouched low, looking tentatively back towards the caravans. The men were nowhere to be seen. She hugged the briefcase to her chest, relieved and excited that it had come to no harm.

She paused a while longer, then made her way up through the field towards the woodland, glancing about her at all times. She reached the fence and checked again that no-one followed. Then she hopped over and gambolled gratefully into the comforting embrace of the trees. Here she felt as safe as if she were behind a locked door. Nobody came to her woodland. Nobody trod its paths. Nobody knew of the hidden cave she had made her den.

Within a minute or so she had reached it. Lou could almost have cried with relief. She pushed the briefcase to the very back of it. She had no wish to try opening it without the others. That would not be fair. She felt anxious about them and hoped they were ok.

Lou put her tin kettle on the stove and sent Jack a text while it boiled. Within seconds he replied: *'All fine, glad u ok. Come round 4 tea, you're invited, 6.30pm. M and D know nothing, so careful wot u say.'*

Lou smiled.

Clack! Joe the crow alighted in the cave entrance.

'Hello Joe,' said Lou. 'You'll never guess what I've been up to today!'

CHAPTER EIGHT

Amazing discovery

WHEN Lou arrived at the caravan, the evening meal was bubbling away in a large casserole pot. It smelt delicious. It was a long-time family favourite concocted by Paul Johnson years ago – steak cooked in wine, flavoured with herbs, spices and garlic, topped with melted macaroni cheese and served with fries.

'I wish my parents could cook like this,' said Lou to Mr and Mrs Johnson in the kitchen. 'They just heat ready-meals up in the microwave. It gets boring after a while.'

Mrs Johnson smiled. 'Well I hope you're still hungry after that huge barbecue you had at lunchtime, the others have told us all about your exciting trip to the islands.'

Lou glanced at Jack. No, it was ok; his parents clearly didn't know quite how exciting their afternoon had turned out.

'That's right, Mrs Johnson, it was an action-packed day,' replied Lou. 'We all had a great time.'

Jack went to the window and looked out. There was no-one about. He ached to speak to Lou without his parents overhearing. 'I might take the dogs a quick walk before tea if that's ok. I could do with the fresh air.'

'Ok,' said his dad. 'They've already been a long walk this afternoon, but I'm sure they won't object.'

To their parents' surprise, all the children, including David, trooped out with the dogs. They walked as quickly as they could along the circular road through the site then up the steep lane to the headland above.

'Fresh air? They've been out in the fresh air all day. And they hardly ever take those dogs a walk,' marvelled Mrs Johnson. 'That Lou is a miracle worker!'

The headland gave a useful bird's eye view of the caravans below and the road network between them. The children scanned carefully for any sign of the men, but there was nothing.

'The case – is it safe?' asked Jack in a low voice.

Lou nodded. 'Tell me what happened after I ran off with it,' she asked him. 'I hated clearing off like that but it was our only chance.'

'You were a genius to split away like that, Lou,' said Jack, admiringly. 'We were fine, a bit scared, but fine.'

Jack, David and Emily recounted how the men pounced on them and ordered them to hand over the case.

'We told them we hadn't got it, then they demanded to know what we were hiding beneath the rug. It was just the rucksack of course,' said Jack.

'It was frightening,' added Emily, 'but we just played dumb. Then they grabbed hold of the rug and snatched it away. When they could see we didn't have the case they got angry. They then realised you weren't with us and kept saying "where's your friend gone, you tell us where she is." One of them cleared off after you and we just ignored the other one. Then he went off searching for you as well.'

Lou smiled. 'You were very brave. David, were these the same men you saw talking on the beach yesterday, or can't you be sure?'

'It was definitely them – Mick and Griffo,' said David. 'Both stumpy with round arms, dark, greasy hair and fat tummies. Mick has tattoos on his arms and Griffo wears a gold earring in one ear.'

'I got to see them too, from underneath a caravan, although I didn't get a great view of them,' said Lou. 'I was hoping to run straight through the site, up the field and into my woodland den but I hesitated a moment too long and had to hide instead. I dived under a caravan, thinking it was empty but it wasn't. It belonged to an elderly couple who came out to take afternoon tea on the patio.'

The others' eyes opened wide as she explained how she nearly got caught by the smugglers but was discovered instead by the elderly couple who outfoxed the men and helped save her from them. They laughed at hearing how she then took tea and scones with them.

'It was all very civilised,' joked Lou. 'But I was lucky, things could have turned out very differently. Anyway, no harm done, we've got the case and it's now safely at the back of my cave, ready for us to open. I can't wait! We've done really well but listen everybody, we must be ultra-careful from now on. Those men might well return to this caravan site to look for us. They are bound to think that we are staying here.

'Our big advantage is that there are hundreds of cara-vans and chalets, and they have no idea which one you are staying in. Nor will they have any idea where my cottage is. We must keep it that way. We must make sure we are never seen going to or from your parents' caravan. Nor must we walk along the main road through the site. We should come and go via this headland.'

The others nodded solemnly.

The children didn't stay out long. They had no wish to risk bumping into those men again. Apart from that they were also very hungry. The dogs were happy enough with their extra walk, though. They panted alongside the children as they returned. They had never had so much exercise!

'Meal will be about another 15 minutes,' called Mrs Johnson from the kitchen.

The children sat down in the lounge where Mr Johnson was watching the news on TV.

'Ten men were arrested by police and customs officers when they stepped off the ferry at Holyhead today. They

are suspected of being members of an international smuggling ring bringing contraband into the UK through the ports of Dublin and Holyhead. A spokesman for HM Revenue and Customs said today the smugglers saw Ireland as the weak link for their activities in the UK.'

The picture cut to an interview with a Customs man:
'These arrests send out a clear warning to those engaged in criminal activities that police and customs in both the UK and Ireland are now watching these ports like hawks. Anyone bringing in illegal goods through Holyhead faces the prospect of being caught, prosecuted and given a lengthy jail sentence.'

'I say, guys,' said Mr Johnson, grinning, 'sounds like the smugglers are still at large then! That reminds me, did you manage to find the hidden loot earlier? I bet you've had a bit of teasing over that today, haven't you, David?'

None of the children said a word. They sat there, dumbstruck, staring at the TV. David's story had sounded farfetched, but had turned out completely true. And now on the news, was a report of smugglers arrested at a North Wales port not that far from Abersoch. Suddenly, smuggling seemed only too real to Lou, Jack, David and Emily.

'Meal's ready,' called Mrs Johnson from the kitchen, interrupting an awkward silence. 'Come on everybody. Well, Lou, I hope you like it. My husband was supposed to be cooking tonight – it's his recipe after all. So if it isn't quite up to the usual standard, then that's his fault.'

'Sorry, love, I was busy chatting to the kids,' said Mr Johnson. 'Not that they have much to say for themselves tonight, do you?'

'Oh leave them alone,' said his wife. 'They're probably worn out after all that sailing.'

'Anyway, team, what plans have you got for tomorrow?' he asked, determined to get some conversation out of them. 'Are you off on an expedition or do you want to come with your mum and me? We're going to Portmeirion for the day – the Italian village near Porthmadog.'

Mr Johnson paused for a moment before adding: 'Oh that's a thought, they don't allow dogs so we could do with someone staying put to look after them. I take it that will be you, David?'

'We'll all stay put if that's ok,' said Jack, glad for an excuse not to go. 'Don't worry about the dogs, we'll give them plenty of exercise.'

~~~~~

The following morning after another huge cooked breakfast, Paul and Liz Johnson set off in the car for Portmeirion. They would be gone most of the day. Jack, David and Emily waved their parents goodbye, put the dogs on the lead, and set off for Lou's woodland den.

'Hello you lot,' said Lou with a smile, as they pushed their way through the curtain of ferns and bracken concealing her secret hide-out.

The kettle was already boiling away on the stove.

'Tea first, then down to business,' said Lou, her emerald eyes gleaming with anticipation.

There, in the middle of the cave floor, was the mysterious leather briefcase.

'I've been guarding it all night,' said Lou, as she handed out mugs of tea. She often slept in the cave if she felt like it.

'It's locked, and we don't have a key,' said Emily. 'How are we going to open it?'

'We'll probably have to hack into it with a knife,' said Lou. 'Well, we're not planning to return it to those men, are we? How else are we going to open it?'

'I don't know if we should do that,' said Emily, 'it seems wrong.'

'So is smuggling,' retorted Lou. 'Look, do you want to know what's inside or not? I'll cut the case open, then you can blame me if you want! Or would you like to?' she said, turning to David.

Everyone agreed that it should be Lou, since it was her quick mind and good sense which had saved the day. The others stared transfixed as the resourceful youngster produced a sharp Stanley knife and thrust it into the front of the briefcase.

'Here goes,' she said.

It was no easy task. The leather ripped easily but the blade struggled to pierce the tough inner casing.

'You have a go, Jack,' she said.

Both Jack and David took turns with Lou at sawing through the stubborn fabric. It was very hard work. Eventually, after about half an hour, they had managed to gouge out a large enough hole to look inside. They could hardly breathe with excitement.

Lou fished out a newspaper, the *Irish Independent*. So this case had come from Ireland! That was interesting, bearing in mind what they had seen on the news the previous day. But there was nothing else.

The children stared into the plush, cream-coloured interior, looking into every corner.

'It's empty! There's nothing else, I'm afraid,' said Lou.

'There must be,' said David.

'There isn't,' said Jack.

For several seconds, nobody spoke. Lou, Jack, David and Emily simply sat there, staring at the now hopelessly wrecked briefcase and its sole contents: an old newspaper.

'How unbelievably disappointing,' said David, looking miserable.

'It doesn't make sense,' said Lou. 'Why bury a case with nothing in it save for a boring old newspaper?'

She took the newspaper and gave it a shake, then opened its pages one by one. After all, there might be something hidden inside it.

But there wasn't.

'Right,' said Lou, looking at the others' dejected faces. 'Well, there's no point moping about it. Perhaps this wasn't the smugglers' case after all. It might just have been discarded junk, who knows? Let's clear up the mess and put it in a bin bag so we can throw it away without anyone asking questions.'

'May I have another quick look, first,' said Emily timidly.

She pressed her fingers around the inner sides of the briefcase and against the back. She had very petite, sensitive hands and the fabric seemed unusually springy to the touch.

'May I borrow the knife a minute?'

Lou, looking doubtful, handed her the knife. 'Be ever so careful, it's really sharp.'

Emily gently ran the blade along all four edges of the base, cutting through the suede backing. She pulled it away. The case was not empty, after all. There was a package of some kind wrapped in bubble-wrap plastic and bound with Sellotape. The others looked on, wide-eyed in astonishment. Emily handed the package to Lou, who gave it her back.

'This is your find, Emily, you open it,' she said.

Carefully, without rushing, Emily's dainty fingers pulled the bubble-wrap open. There, in front of them, were several bundles of paper, like neatly-printed vouchers. Emily removed one and held it up for them all to see. It was rather dim in the cave so they went to the entrance in order to view it properly in natural light.

In each corner was the number 100. In the middle was an old-fashioned portrait of a man with a name underneath – Franklin.

'That will be Benjamin Franklin,' whispered David. 'He was one of the founding fathers of the United States.

We read about him in history at school.'

Across the top, in capitals, were the words FEDERAL RESERVE NOTE and THE UNITED STATES OF AMERICA. Across the bottom: ONE HUNDRED DOLLARS.

'*This note is legal tender for all debts, public and private*,' read David.

'Money!' exclaimed Jack. 'American money. Let's check the other bundles and see if they're the same.'

They returned to the cave. Each of them picked up a wad of banknotes, bound with an elastic band, and looked at them carefully. They all appeared to be identical.

The children looked at each other in wonder, too stunned to speak. They ran their fingers over the edges of the notes, spellbound. They had no idea how much they were all worth, but knew instinctively that it was a small fortune.

Eventually, Emily spoke, a small frown crossing her face. 'The money is foreign, it can't be used here in England, can it?'

'I'll tell Eifion you said that,' grinned Lou. 'We're in Wales, not England!'

'It's still proper money, just like our pounds and pence,' said Jack. 'These notes could easily be exchanged for English money at banks.'

Jack flipped over the note in his hand. On the reverse was a large, impressive building which he thought looked familiar, and the inscription '*The United States of America, In God We Trust, One Hundred Dollars.*'

'How many bundles are there in total?' asked Lou. 'We must be careful to keep them together. We don't want any blowing away in the wind.'

They counted them carefully: there were thirty.

'I've got a calculator on my mobile phone,' said Jack. 'I can work out more or less exactly how much this lot is worth if each wad contains the same number of notes and if they're all for one hundred dollars each.'

Emily counted the one she was holding. 'There are fifty in this one and they all say one hundred dollars.

The others counted a bundle each and got the same result.

'Right, thirty bundles multiplied by fifty notes equals one thousand, five hundred notes. And one thousand, five hundred multiplied by one hundred dollars means there is, hang on.' Jack tapped the figures into the calculator. 'A total of one hundred and fifty thousand American dollars.'

'I think,' said David, 'that a dollar is worth about sixty pence. So if you multiply one hundred and fifty thousand by nought point six, then you've got what all this lot is worth in pounds.'

Jack didn't quite understand why he should multiply by nought point six but David was good at maths so he took his word for it. 'Ok,' he said, 'that makes ninety thousand pounds.'

'Ninety thousand pounds!' gasped Emily, 'oh wow, that's massive! What could you buy for that? A house or something?'

'A small one, just about. Or four really nice cars,' said David.

'What's more,' said Jack, 'we have stumbled across just one case. Imagine how many more they are no doubt bringing in, stuffed with American money! No wonder they were so cross when they realised we'd discovered their precious case.'

'It wouldn't only have been the loss of this case which bothered the smugglers,' said Lou, thoughtfully. 'It's that if it got handed over to the police, the authorities will know what they are now up to. These men have already had to change their plans once. Remember the news last night – the ports are all guarded, smugglers are being caught as they go through customs. So instead of walking into a trap at Holyhead, they are trying to land their goods on the British mainland where there are no customs officers – places like Abersoch or Whistling Sands. They want to sail their valuable cargo across in boats in the dead of night hoping to come ashore without anyone seeing them!'

The others looked at her, their faces solemn.

'Well think about it,' continued Lou. 'If you were a smuggler where would you prefer to land? A port where police and customs officers are watching your every move and scanning your luggage for anything suspicious, or a dark little beach with no-one about?'

The children paused for a minute as they sought to take it all in. It turned out that the men whom they had light-heartedly referred to as smugglers really were exactly that – and not just colourful rascals bringing in a few bottles of illicit whisky or something similar but serious criminals involved in a very lucrative operation of some kind.

'As Lou was saying,' said Jack, 'these people may now fear that if this case is handed to the police, the whole coastline will be watched. They *were* going to use Whistling Sands or somewhere like that, but they may now change their plans completely.'

'But remember,' said David, 'Griffo and Mick have already messed up one delivery. If they change their strategy again, the ringleaders of their gang will want to know why. They aren't going to want to admit that one of their cases has been discovered by kids and that the police are on their trail. Also, they don't know I overheard their conversation. They don't know that we have a very good idea which beach they plan to use. At a guess, they'll want to stick with Whistling Sands because it has such an excellent get-away road right down to the beach itself.'

'I think you're right, David, although they will proba-bly delay a while to let the dust settle,' said Lou. 'They will watch and wait to see if the authorities appear to be taking action. If nothing happens, they will go ahead as planned. We now have to decide what to do. I believe we ought to try and find out as much as we can about these men first. In the meantime, this money stays hidden, safe at the back of the den, and we do not breathe a word to anyone!'

Emily could not see how they could possibly find out anything but Lou had a good idea. Her father's laptop computer could easily be connected to the internet. They could go online and search for information.

Lou rang the cottage. Her mother answered the phone, sounding bad tempered as usual. Her father was out on a job and no, her mother did not want the house 'crowded out' with Lou and her new friends.

'I'll just pop round myself then and borrow dad's laptop. Then I'll be out of your way,' retorted Lou, determined not to be put off.

'Well you make sure you get it back before he's home,' snapped Mrs Elliott. 'He'll need that to write his story up to sell and we need every penny we can get at the moment.'

The girl sighed as she ended the call. How typical. Her mother was always in a mood and her father was always too busy to bother with her. It was a pity her parents were not more like Mr and Mrs Johnson!

CHAPTER NINE

On the smugglers' trail

LOU slipped away to her parents' cottage to pick up her father's laptop. While she was gone, the others took the dogs a walk through the woods. They felt safe with trees all around them. The smugglers would never find them here!

'There's something about woodland isn't there,' said Emily looking at the treetops above. 'It's so calm and peaceful.'

They stopped for a moment to listen to the whispering branches and birds chattering overhead. They were soothing sounds, which helped the children to feel more relaxed and composed. Their incredible discovery earlier had rattled them somewhat. It had been immensely exciting but disconcerting at the same time.

Jack and David, in particular, felt a touch ill at ease that the four of them were all now custodians of a huge stockpile of American banknotes which did not belong to them. Was Lou right to store them at the back of her cave for the time being without immediately telling a grown-up? On the other hand, reflected Jack, there was more chance of Lou getting things right than the rest of them. If anyone knew exactly what she was doing, Lou Elliott did.

The dogs enjoyed their time in the woods, too, dashing after sticks and chasing each other around. Barney discovered something interesting up a huge, ivy-covered oak and started barking madly. It was almost certainly a squirrel!

'Shush, Barney,' ordered Jack, worried the noise might attract attention.

After a pleasant walk, the children arrived back at the

den at the same time as Lou.

'That was well-timed!' she said.

The others watched as Lou swiftly connected her mobile phone to the laptop.

'The computer will now connect to the internet via the mobile,' she said proudly. She loved showing off to the others and teaching them new tricks.

Fancy having internet access in their little den!

Lou logged onto the net and opened a search engine. 'Now, think of some key words to search on,' she said. 'Remember the story we heard on the news last night and what we've discovered today.'

The children gathered round the screen and concentrated hard. One by one, they began to shout out useful words: Smuggling, Ireland, Dublin, Money. Lou typed them into the search engine. The computer immediately found more than one hundred thousand entries.

'Far too many,' said Lou. 'Come on, think of more, we need to narrow it down a bit.'

'Dollars,' said Emily, suddenly.

'Of course! Well done Emily,' said Lou. 'We should have thought of that straightaway.'

The computer still found an incredible seventy-three thousand pages containing these words. The children looked in disappointment at each other. They could hardly read through all those!

'It's hopeless,' said David, usually the first to give up.

'No it isn't,' said Lou, 'I think this could be what we are looking for. Look! Second story down – something about superdollars and money moved to Dublin.'

'And the next one,' cried Jack – the counterfeit cash is then smuggled to Dublin, from Ireland it's taken to . . .'

The summary ended there and Lou clicked on the story to bring the rest up. It contained the text of a BBC TV programme about the 'Superdollar'. The young children could not fully understand everything but it was clearly about criminals smuggling American money into Britain via Ireland.

'The highest quality counterfeit notes ever produced,' read out Jack. 'The forgeries are so realistic that even the experts can't tell the difference. Britain and Ireland were being flooded with counterfeit cash.'

'Excuse me for being thick,' said Emily, 'but I don't understand what counterfeit means.'

Nor did Jack and David, but they were too proud to admit it.

'It means that the money being smuggled is fake,' answered Lou. 'It's not real money, it's essentially worthless.'

'What about the money we found? Is that worthless, too? Oh what a shame,' said Emily. 'Just think what we could have bought with it.'

'Don't be silly, Emily,' said Jack. 'We couldn't spend the money anyway, it isn't ours to spend.'

'But why call these dollars *super* if they aren't real? They don't seem very super to me,' said Emily.

'Because they are super *copies*,' replied Lou. 'They are so perfect they are even fooling the experts. And if they are that good, they can be spent exactly like real ones – and these criminals can print countless hundreds of them. In that sense, they are better than real banknotes, because they can produce huge numbers of them.'

'How do we know whether the ones we found are fakes or the real thing?' asked David.

'We don't,' said Lou. 'It's impossible to know for sure. But it seems to fit in with what we have just found out: a large quantity of banknotes, all the same value and – did you notice – all in perfect, mint condition. Anyway, real or counterfeit, the people behind this racket are involved in major international crime with a great deal of explaining to do should they ever get caught.'

'But where are these dollars coming from, and why are

they being brought here from Ireland?' asked David.

Lou glanced at the screen. The battery indicator was well over half empty. 'We've got about another thirty minutes to find that out before the power goes.'

The children fell silent and gathered again around the laptop. There was no time to lose. Lou search the website they were looking at for references to Holyhead, the North Wales port mentioned in the news item. It found a match. According to the website, two men arrived at Holyhead off the ferry from Ireland with counterfeit dollar notes stuffed inside the lining of their coats.

The others watched as Lou expertly skimmed the document on the screen, her sharp eyes moving quickly down the page.

'What have you found, Lou?' asked Jack, unable to contain himself any longer.

'It says the superdollars are collected in the Russian capital, Moscow, by an Irish gang. They take them back to Ireland, but then bring them over to Britain. They want to turn the fake dollars into real money as quickly as possible, so they cart them to loads of banks all over the place and exchange them.'

'Why not do that in Ireland, why bring them here?' asked David.

Lou paused. 'I suppose it's easier to get rid of fake money over here. Ireland is a much smaller country than Britain and taking large amounts of American cash to banks there might look suspicious.'

'Of course!' said Jack, as the penny dropped. 'That makes perfect sense. But as we said before, Customs officials are on to them, and watching as they board the big ferries from Ireland to Britain. So instead, these criminals are switching to sailing their own boats across the Irish Sea packed with superdollars and landing at deserted beaches and coves in the dead of night, when no-one's about!'

The boy got up, stiff after sitting so long. 'Only now, WE shall be watching,' Jack declared, eyes lighting up. 'Beware, you smugglers, we know your game and we're coming after you!'

'All right Jack, don't get carried away,' warned Lou, mindful that Emily looked rather scared.

Lou glanced at a few other websites. One, belonging to an American newspaper, told of a gang in Ireland being investigated for smuggling counterfeit banknotes worth millions of dollars into their country from Russia, then transferring them to Britain through Holyhead and on to the West Midlands. She searched again, this time including words such as Abersoch, Aberdaron, the Lleyn peninsula. Nothing! Perhaps no-one knew that these people had hit upon a new way of importing their illegal cargo. No-one knew, that is, except a bunch of children. Lou shivered slightly.

Suddenly a high-pitched beep made the children jump. Jack grabbed David in fright and Emily screamed. Even Lou looked startled. But then she said, with a sheepish smile, 'don't worry, it's the laptop. It beeps when the battery's nearly flat. Time's up I'm afraid, folks.'

Lou closed the computer down carefully, anxious to leave no clue to what they had used it for. She checked her watch – her father would be back soon, she should return it quickly. She left the others still debating in the cave.

'You know, I really think we ought to tell mum and dad,' said Emily, after Lou had gone. 'We must hand over this money. We can't keep it, it's dangerous.'

Jack looked thoughtful. 'It's like we said earlier, if we do that, the police will be on the case immediately. They'll comb the area, patrol cars will be sent to the caravan site, there'll be police boats all round the coast; officers on our local beach and at Whistling Sands. 'The smugglers will be spooked and clear off.'

'Would that be such a bad thing?' asked Emily. 'We don't exactly want them round for tea, do we?'

'Don't you want to catch these people?' snapped Jack, impatiently. 'As children we won't be half so easy to spot as policemen. We can snoop around on our bikes, on foot and by boat and we'll look like what we are – kids on holiday. If we don't get anywhere – we hand the super-dollars to the police.'

'Yes, but those smugglers have seen us, don't forget,' said Emily, unconvinced. 'They would recognise us and for all we know, they're still planning to come after us.'

Surprisingly, David came to Jack's aid. 'They have only seen us through binoculars, running away across the beach,' he said. 'They've never seen Lou up close and when they caught us three we were all wearing caps and sunglasses.'

Jack pondered then said, 'I think there's some risk they will recognise us round here, but anywhere else they probably wouldn't make the connection. What is vital, as we said before, is that they don't know which caravan we're staying in.'

Then something else struck him. 'If we tell police straightaway, the smugglers will guess it was us who told them! That could put us in even more danger and perhaps lead to our parents having to take us home.'

It was not an appealing thought.

'Anyway, we shouldn't think of doing anything without discussing it with Lou first,' insisted Jack. The others agreed.

His phone beeped. It was a text from Lou. The laptop was back safely, and did they want to go for a bike ride to Whistling Sands the following day 'for a swim and sunbathe and a prowl around.'

Emily and David exchanged glances.

'Oh don't worry,' reassured Jack. 'We'll take our

swimming things, a rug, a few towels and a barbecue and have a great day out. We won't come to any harm with Lou at our side and it will get us out of Abersoch for a bit.'

CHAPTER TEN

Day out at Whistling Sands

LOU called round at 6.30am as they wanted an early start. They would be less likely to be seen at that time and also, Mr and Mrs Johnson needed them back by 7.30pm for a family meal out. Lou had been pleased to be invited too. She was almost feeling part of the Johnson family by now. The girl felt happier than for a long time as she and the others slipped discreetly out of the caravan site via the headland, then mounted their bikes and pedalled away along an empty road, bound for Whistling Sands.

It was certain to be another hot summer's day but at that hour, the air was refreshingly cool. The children turned right on the approach to Abersoch and groaned as they cycled up the steep hill. It was too much for Emily and David who were forced to walk.

'Don't worry,' said Lou. 'Once we're past the turning for Mynytho it's easier. Anyway the exercise will do you good!'

There seemed to be no-one about as they rode west towards their destination near the tip of the Lleyn peninsula, save for the occasional tractor and Land Rover.

'I love it at this time in the morning,' enthused David. 'Everything feels so fresh and new. It's great to be up and about doing things while everybody else is in bed.'

Jack laughed. 'Yes, David, you're always up and about at this time, aren't you?'

Everybody chuckled at that, including David. A few days earlier, he would have sulked but was learning to take a little friendly teasing.

'Have you noticed how the cows in the fields look up in

surprise as we go past?' said Emily. 'They're not used to seeing people so early.'

'They're looking surprised that David is with us,' joked Jack.

Round one particularly muddy bend they came to a halt. The road was full of sheep being moved from one field to another. A black and white collie was doing an expert job of rounding them up.

'Barney would enjoy that,' remarked Jack. 'He would make a great sheep dog.'

'You see so much more, don't you, when you walk or cycle,' observed Emily as they rode through the village of Sarn Meyllteyrn. 'Look at the wildflowers in the hedge-rows – I hardly ever notice them in a car. Mmm, can you smell that wonderful wild honeysuckle? Oh and a tiny pottery shop!' She pointed ahead to a rustic-looking building, freshly-painted in a garish bright blue and pink.

'Well we're too early, it won't be open yet,' said Jack, knowing his sister would love to go in and browse.

Round another corner and it was 'oooh' again – Emily had spotted a handwritten sign advertising fresh crab for sale. 'Can we take a quick detour and buy some?'

'Sorry about Emily, Lou,' said Jack. 'We won't bring her again.'

Lou smiled. 'I love crab, too! The fishermen often give me a free one when they empty the lobster pots. We could do with a snack on the way. I know the chap who sells them – he'll be up and about by now.'

So they turned down a narrow, winding lane to buy fresh, dressed crab. It looked very tasty. The children then cycled on for several more miles through the gentle rolling farmland of the Lleyn peninsula. Now and again, they caught a glimpse of the sea to both the north and south. Shortly after the village of Penygroeslon, they came to a copse of trees.

'Let's stop for a quick break,' said Lou. They leaned

their bikes against an ancient-looking wooden gatepost and sat on the dry grass.

'Crab anyone?' asked Lou with a grin. With crusty bread and washed down with lemonade it was delicious.

'Another twenty minutes and we'll be there,' said Lou as they got under way.

The children arrived at Whistling Sands not much after 9am. There were already a few people about.

'You see how easy it would be to pick up cargo from this beach?' said Lou as they walked down the steep asphalt road to the shore. 'There would be no problem getting quite a large van down here, turning it round, loading it, then away! I'm sure this is the beach they mean.'

The children stepped onto the sand and stared out at the rich blue sea, flecked with the white foam of breaking waves. A long way off, they noticed a couple of boats.

'Could they be smugglers?' asked Emily, half seriously, half joking.

'Maybe,' replied Lou, 'who knows? Maybe those windsurfers are smugglers. Let's not do too much staring and pointing for now, ok? Let's focus on being holiday-makers.'

The children found themselves a good spot at the foot of the dunes, changed into their swimwear, raced each other to the sea and threw themselves in. The surf was always much stronger this side of the peninsula than at Abersoch. The sea pounded the shore with towering ice-cold, white-crested waves which crashed over the children making them gasp for breath.

When they'd worked up an appetite they ran back up the beach and dried off quickly under the hot sun now rising in a cloudless sky. Lou got the barbecue going. It was soon belching out thick, aromatic smoke.

'Mmm, I love the smell of charcoal,' she said, grabbing

the tongs. 'Ok, what shall I put on first – spare ribs, sausage, bacon, chicken drumsticks or a bit of everything?'

When they were filled to bursting, they spread towels out over the soft, warm sand and flopped. Lou got her book out and started reading.

'I wonder why they call this beach *Whistling Sands*,' asked Emily, lying on her back and burrowing her feet into the sand.

'Because the sand squeaks under your feet when you walk on it,' replied Lou.

Jack was restless. His head buzzed with their discovery the previous day. He was keen to explore the shore and the overhanging cliffs for clues.

'Lou, shall I scout around for signs of anything strange?' he asked her.

'I'll come too,' offered David.

'Ok, you pair go off and scout around, then report back,' said Lou, fighting the urge to smile. 'Actually it's less suspicious than if we're all together. I'll keep watch here.' She snuggled into her towel and buried her head back in her book.

'I can't get the sand to squeak at all,' said Emily. 'I wonder why it's supposed to squeak more here than on other beaches?'

'Oh shush a bit will you, I'm trying to read,' replied Lou, impatiently. 'I've just got to another really exciting bit.'

'I thought you said you were keeping watch? Cos if so, you're facing the wrong way,' said Emily.

'Emily, I tell you what, *you* keep watch for a bit. For now, I'm reading my book, ok?' retorted Lou.

'I suppose your life's exciting enough anyway, isn't it?' persisted Emily, refusing to take the hint.

Lou sighed and put her book down. She was evidently

not going to get any peace. 'If you think living with my parents is exciting, think again,' she said.

As Emily clearly wanted to chat, Lou told her how dull and lonely life could sometimes be growing up in rural Shropshire, with no brothers or sisters and few friends living close – and parents who spent no time with her.

Emily looked at her sympathetically.

'Don't feel sorry for me, it's not that terrible. I'd rather live where I do than in the middle of a noisy town,' said Lou. 'I enjoy my own company and make my own fun. I'm perfectly happy most of the time but sometimes it can be a bit desolate, especially when it rains. But I never mope – if I feel fed up I go for a brisk walk over the hills nearby and don't come back until I'm feeling cheerful.'

'Also, you've always got holidays at Abersoch to look forward to,' said Emily. 'And you're not on your own here any more – you've got us.'

'I love coming here and I'm really pleased we've all become friends,' said Lou. 'It's great. I just hope . . .' Her voice trailed off and suddenly she looked sad.

'Go on,' said Emily. 'What do you hope? What's the matter, Lou?'

'To be honest, I'm not sure how long we will be able to keep coming here. Dad's writing isn't going well. He's a freelance journalist meaning he works for several different newspapers but they all seem to be cutting back on using outside staff. He's finding it harder and harder to make a living. As for my mum, she's bone idle. She does nothing all day but lounge about in front of the TV. I'm a bit worried, you know.'

Lou's eyes looked shiny as if they were filling with tears. It was most unlike her.

Emily reached out and gave her arm a squeeze. 'I hope things work out. And remember that you can come and stay with us any time – at our home in Cheshire or at Abersoch. Don't get upset, Lou, I always think of you as so strong and independent. And you seem to have a way of sensing what's about to happen. Like the other day, on the island. You knew something was wrong; that we were being watched.'

Lou smiled. 'I saw sunlight reflecting off those men's binoculars. I guessed they were spying on us. It was no more than that, just a hunch, that's all. I've learnt to trust my instincts.'

'I wish I had your talents,' said Emily.

'You have your *own* talents,' pointed out Lou, earnestly. 'Don't seek to be like me – I'm a wild child who's had to grow up fast, too fast maybe. You're a much gentler person than me, and there's nothing wrong with that.'

The boys arrived back, empty-handed. They had scoured the beach thoroughly for signs of anything untoward. At one point, Jack thought he had seen the sides of a case from beneath a pile of seaweed, but it turned out to be a rotting crate. They had found a dead jellyfish and a dogfish washed up on the shore. They had even examined the cliffs and checked the vehicles parked on the grass at the top for signs of anything suspicious. But there was nothing of interest to report.

Lou didn't seem too troubled. 'Well done for looking so hard,' she told them. 'That was a good effort.'

'So what shall we do now?' asked Jack.

'Chill out and carry on sunbathing. I've got a lot more reading to do, my book's getting quite thrilling now. Oh, I could do with a cup of tea though, if anyone's offering.'

'I'll get you one,' replied the two boys together.

'Yes, and get your sister a cup, too,' said Emily with an amused frown.

Lou had five minutes to get back into her book before Jack gave a cry. 'A flash of sunlight out to sea, from that boat.' He pointed. 'Are they watching us?'

'Don't point, you fool,' reprimanded Lou. She turned

round. It looked like no more than an ordinary sailing dinghy, nothing like the powerful motorboat which came after them the previous day. Nonetheless, she tore herself away from her novel, wrapped her binoculars in a towel and took a look. She saw two men and a woman on board.

'I think I can see a young child as well. They're unlikely to be part of any smuggling gang,' she concluded. 'Those men don't seem the sort to bring their women and children along.'

It looked to be a false alarm. And when Lou, Jack, David and Emily mounted their bicycles for the ride back to Abersoch, they appeared no closer to finding out more about the smugglers. After the dramatic developments of the previous two days, it was rather an anti-climax.

'It's as we thought, they're lying low,' said Lou. 'In any case, the daytime is probably not the ideal time to come. We ought to be here at night, but we have no idea when.'

'So where do we go from here, Lou?' asked David. 'We seem no further forward.'

'We're not, but who cares, we've had a great day out haven't we? What's meant to be is meant to be,' she added, mysteriously. 'We must listen out and look out for a clue to get us back on the smugglers' trail. It may come along when we least expect it and when it does, we must be ready.'

~~~~~

Back in Abersoch, Lou left the others to return home, shower and change for the evening meal with their parents. She locked her bike up outside the cottage and went in. Her mother was on the sofa watching TV and her father was at the dining room table, typing away on his laptop.

'How's it going, dad?' Lou asked. 'Are you working on

an exciting story?'

Her father grunted. 'Can't talk right now, Lou, I've got to get this copy emailed to the newsdesk within the next fifteen minutes if I want paying.'

Lou sat in the armchair and turned to her mother. She tried to tell her about their day at Whistling Sands but she wasn't interested.

'Do you mind, Lou, I'm trying to watch this,' said her mother, waving her hand towards a quiz show on TV.

Lou gave up and went to her room to get ready.

'I don't suppose anyone's interested but I'm going out for a meal tonight with the Johnsons,' she said, heading for the door a few minutes later.

'Well if you're going to be late, try not to make a noise coming in,' replied her mother.

'Have a great time,' said her father. 'Sorry not to chat, I'm just so busy right now.'

Lou left through the back door and took the private path to the beach below. She had a few minutes to spare. She sat on a rock and gazed at the islands and the lighthouse in front of which she and the others had enjoyed a picnic a couple of days earlier. She felt rather flat – why were her parents so cold with her?

She didn't stay low for long. She reminded herself that she had three wonderful new friends and how much more fun life was now. She glanced behind her at the path to their holiday cottage. That was the spot where she had first bumped into Jack. He was a bit of a mummy's boy, despite his denials, but sweet and Lou was fond of him – fond of them all – but particularly Jack. She prayed her father's work would pick up so they could afford to keep coming here.

'Hello missy, *noswaith dda* (good evening),' said a voice.

It was her elderly friend Eifion, out for his evening stroll across the beach. His tanned, wrinkled face broke into a broad smile.

'Hello again,' she said. 'Sorry, I was miles away.'

'I haven't seen you for a while,' the old man said, leaning against his stick.

'I know, it's my new friends, Eifion, they're keeping me busy.'

'Hope they're not getting you into any mischief,' he replied with a wink.

'Other way round I think,' said Lou, winking back.

The pair chatted for a while before Lou looked at her watch, then sprang to her feet. 'I better go – I'm meeting them for a meal tonight with their parents.'

She wished Eifion a pleasant evening and promised to catch up with him properly soon, then jumped onto the sand and walked off towards the Vaynol Arms in the centre of Abersoch.

The others were already there. It was a warm summer's evening and they were seated round a bench on the terrace outside overlooking the road.

'Hello Lou,' said Mr and Mrs Johnson as she turned up, apologising for being late.

'Don't worry, we've only just got here,' said Mrs Johnson. 'Glad you could make it. Sounds like you've had another fun day! Looks like you've caught the sun all of you, too!'

Freckles had come out across Jack and David's now pink faces. Emily's gentle gold complexion had deepened and so too had Lou's more olive features. Lou had changed into a pair of black jeans with a striped blue and white top and a necklace and matching bracelet made from seashells.

The other children looked admiringly at her because she looked so smart and pretty, while they were still in their beach clothes. Going out for a meal was a rare treat for Lou and she wanted to look her best. Mrs Johnson complimented her on her appearance, much to her delight.

'Well, isn't it nice to eat a meal outside and watch the world go by,' said Mrs Johnson, her eyes sweeping up and down the street. 'Oh I say, Paul, will you look at the colour they've painted their window frames.' Mrs Johnson turned to her husband and pointed towards the café opposite called Y Bwtri.

The children looked across at the cheerful lime green frames, trying to work out what was wrong with them. Then David stiffened. There was a man standing right outside in a T-shirt almost the same colour, with a large belly and tattoos across his thick arms. He was thick-set with messy black hair and a scowling, unshaven face.

David had seen him somewhere before . . .

CHAPTER ELEVEN

David loses his appetite

T HE man's chubby fingers jabbed a message into a
mobile phone. David stared at him. It was Mick the
smuggler! He would know those coarse features anywhere.

Jack and Emily, heads buried in the menu, had not
noticed. As for Lou, she did not instantly recognise him
but guessed who it was from David's reaction.

The boy looked uncomfortable. He placed a trembling
hand to his forehead and Lou saw him nervously peeking
through his fingers. This was dangerous! The man might
recognise them, especially if David was going to act
strangely. Griffo and Mick had both seen Jack, David and
Emily up close, after all.

Lou kicked David gently under the table and he looked
up. Her penetrating eyes locked with his and he sensed
her saying to him: *stay calm, act natural*. Lou pretended
to shiver and was about to suggest they go inside when
Mick shoved his phone back into his jeans pocket and
strode straight past them, into the pub.

'Are you cold, Lou?' asked Mrs Johnson. 'We'll go
indoors if you like.'

'No thanks, Mrs Johnson, it was a sudden draught,
that's all. It's great sitting out here. I'll go for the scampi
and chips if that's ok.'

'David, what about you?' asked his mother. 'What's the
matter, you don't look well.'

He didn't. The chilling sight of the smuggler had left
him pale and his hands shook.

'I'm not that hungry, thanks. I'll be ok, honestly.'

'Oh don't pander to him,' said his dad, unkindly. He

had little patience with his younger son and his moods. 'If David doesn't want to eat, that's up to him. I'm fed up with fussing round him all the time. We've come out for a nice family meal and all he can do is sit there and sulk. Just ignore him.'

Jack could never ignore such moments and wanted to get revenge for his brother's teasing during the tomato sauce dispute the other day. He chimed in: 'you're such a baby, David, you really need to grow up.'

David could not believe his ears. This was so unfair. It wasn't his fault one of those horrible smugglers had appeared out of nowhere. He felt very ill at ease. Those men must hate them for running off with their precious briefcase with its extremely valuable contents. And here they were, calmly eating a meal at a pub where one of them was drinking! Was he supposed to feel peckish right now? It was ok for Jack and Emily, they hadn't spotted him. Then an anger welled up in David. He was fed up of being made to feel like a wimp and a stay-at-home. Hadn't his parents noticed how much more adventurous he had become with Lou on the scene?

'I'll have the scampi too,' he said, suddenly finding an inner strength. He began to relax and regain his composure.

Suddenly, out walked Mick, patting his beer belly and striding past them. He didn't even glance in their direction.

'Actually, I'm still feeling a bit funny,' said David immediately. 'I could do with a quick walk.'

'He's being a pain again, don't let him,' carped Jack.

'Thank you, Jack,' said his dad. 'When I want your help I'll ask for it. David, you can go for a quick walk if you're genuinely not feeling well, but you better be back by the time food is served.'

Lou sipped her cola and smiled inwardly. Jack and Emily didn't know what their brother was up to, but she could guess and admired him for it.

David strode boldly after Mick, scarcely able to believe what he was doing, but too angry to be scared any more. How dare Jack and his dad pick on him like that? He would show them!

The overweight smuggler was flagging slightly as the road headed upwards. He paused outside the fish and chip shop, allowing a tempting aroma to waft up his nostrils. David groaned inwardly, partly because the smell of frying made him hungry, too, but also because he realised he would be hopelessly late back to the pub before long.

Luck was on his side. Mick looked at his watch, decided against a chip supper, and continued walking. David lagged a short distance behind. The smuggler went past the main shops and restaurants. It was more dangerous now, there were fewer people about. The boy darted in between a line of parked cars so that if Mick looked back, he would not see him. Where was he going? Did he have a house around here? If so, the boy wanted to see which one. They were approaching a crossroads. Mick turned left.

A few yards down, Mick halted and reached inside his pocket. He pulled out a packet of cigarettes, lit one and began to smoke it where he stood. David jumped into the red phone box on the grass verge for cover and peered through the glass. A last fag before turning in for the night? It looked like it. Mick threw the cigarette butt on the floor, coughed and headed into a drive. The scrunch of gravel could be heard beneath his feet. David left the phone box and scuttled forwards. It led to the Victoria Lodge guest house. So *that's* where the smuggler was staying!

David took cover directly opposite, his gaze fixed on the upstairs rooms. Three had lights on with the curtains drawn; the other three were in darkness. Dusk was falling now, and if one of the unlit rooms happened to be Mick's he would be sure to see its light going on. He glanced at his watch – 9pm. It would surely only take a minute even for a hefty, unfit chap like Mick to heave his way up the stairs. Nearly two minutes ticked by and nothing. Blow! His room must be on the other side.

Disappointed, David straightened up, about to go. Then a light came on in the bedroom second from the left! A burly fellow with a fat belly hanging out beneath a bright green T-shirt walked over to the windows. David dived out of sight. He hadn't had a chance to see any tattoos but there was no mistaking that top nor the rolls of flab it failed to conceal. The guest, who had to be Mick, yanked the curtains roughly together. David got up and walked swiftly off.

The youngster was elated, he felt like he was worth a million dollars, never mind the one hundred and fifty thousand stashed in Lou's den. The smugglers' trail had gone cold, but thanks to him it had suddenly hotted up again! They now knew where one of them was staying and which room he was in. That was very valuable information. David returned to the Vaynol feeling extremely pleased with himself.

Unfortunately that sentiment was not shared by his father, who brought him sharply down to earth. 'Where have you been?' Mr Johnson demanded angrily. 'You've been gone over half an hour. I told you to be back here in time to eat with us. You clearly had no intention to. I'm most annoyed with you. You've spoilt the meal.'

'We were worried about you, David,' said his mum. 'It's really very selfish of you.'

Jack was about to launch into a scornful dig of his own when he caught Lou's stony-faced stare which he could tell said: *shut up.* The others were scraping their plates and a barmaid came to take them away. David began wolfing his cold scampi, surprisingly hungry now.

'Mmm, this is really good, even though it's cold,' he

announced, with a wide grin. 'Sorry I was so long, I feel much better now, though.'

'What are you so cocky about?' demanded Jack, suspiciously, aware that his sensitive brother usually sulked for hours after a telling off.

'Oooh, wouldn't you like to know,' came the maddening reply.

Even more annoyingly, Lou smiled back, as if she was in on the secret.

Just before bedtime, Jack received a text from Lou, summoning them to a meeting in the den at 10am the following day. She added that they just might be back on the smugglers' trail! Yet surely they had drawn a total blank that day? Jack was perplexed.

What did she mean?

CHAPTER TWELVE

Lou takes a gamble

THE day after, Jack and the others listened intently in the den as David breathlessly recounted his adventure of the night before. Nobody accused him of making up stories this time.

'Fantastic!' said Jack. 'I'm sorry I had a go at you last night.'

It was a rare apology and David, hero of the hour, accepted gracefully.

'David did brilliantly,' said Lou. 'We now have an important new lead but we have to decide what to do with it.'

'I know,' said Emily, suddenly. 'There might be valuable clues in the smuggler's bedroom. Maybe we could get in there and take a look around when he's out?'

'Ok then Emily, do let us know how you get on,' teased Lou, as Emily turned pale. 'Don't worry, I was only joking. You are right, it's what we must do. I think it's a job for me. It will be easier for a girl than you boys.'

'Well I'm a girl and I'm willing to try,' offered Emily, timidly.

Lou smiled. 'No, not this time, but thanks anyway. I will go and David can come with me to point me in the right direction.'

Later that morning, Lou and David walked into Abersoch wearing sunglasses and caps pulled low to disguise their appearance. As they approached the hotel, David began to get cold feet. How could Lou possibly get inside an almost certainly locked guest's bedroom? Lou wondered that too, but didn't let on.

'It will be ok, we've got to be cunning that's all,' she

said. 'I'm good at being cunning!'

The children looked up at the upper floor of the hotel. David pointed out Mick's room, second from the left on the first floor. His curtains were open. That was good, he must be up. But was he out?

'Right, you walk on a bit and keep watch on the hotel window,' said Lou to David. 'If I manage to get inside his room I'll come to the window. Give me a thumbs up to confirm I'm in the right room and thumbs down if it's wrong. See you soon.'

Lou walked nimbly to the front entrance. The main door was ajar so she went straight in. No-one was about. The hum of a vacuum cleaner could be heard from somewhere. The girl poked her head round the corner. A plump cleaning lady was hoovering a threadbare carpet in the dining room, perspiration glistening on her forehead. She hadn't noticed Lou.

'Is the owner available?' Lou shouted over the din of the vacuum cleaner, eventually getting her attention.

'She's out shopping for more bacon,' replied the cleaner, switching it off. 'We ran out this morning again, half the guests went without their breakfast. Memory like a sieve she's got. I'm fed up with this place,' she continued, rubbing her back as she straightened herself up. 'There's supposed to be three of us on today, the other two have rung in sick, and where's the bloomin' owner? This place is falling apart I tell you. Look at it.'

'You're right. I went without breakfast this morning, it's just not good enough. Anyway, I better get off to my room. Nice chatting, don't work too hard,' said Lou, pretending to be a guest.

The cleaner grunted.

Lou climbed the wooden staircase from the dining room to the floor above. Well why not? That cleaner would neither know nor care if she really was a guest. The stairs led to a forlorn landing with dark, dusty walls turned a deep yellow by years of cigarette smoke. A single low-power electric bulb with no shade dangled from a wire, emitting a weak light. There were about half a dozen doors on both sides of the landing, each with tatty brass numbers screwed into them.

Lou tried to get her bearings; it was difficult as there were no windows.

This must be the one, she thought, looking at the door numbered '8'. It was the second one along facing the road. She had no way of knowing whether the smuggler was inside. There was only one thing for it. She pulled her cap down to obscure as much of her face as possible, and knocked smartly on the door. If he answered, she would bluff she had the wrong room. Oh heck, she thought. This could go badly wrong, she was acting too fast, not thinking things through.

There was no reply. Thank goodness! She slowly turned the large, old-fashioned doorknob, and gave the door a gentle push. It would not budge.

Lou returned downstairs to find the cleaner, now in the lobby. 'My dad's got our room key,' she fibbed. 'But he's fallen asleep on the beach. You couldn't lend me a spare, could you? It's room eight on the first floor, second on the right. I just need to nip up and get my sun tan lotion, that's all.'

The cleaner hesitated, about to say no.

'It's getting that hot today I'm afraid I might burn in this weather. I've got terribly sensitive skin,' added Lou, untruthfully. She actually tanned very well.

'Oh go on then,' said the cleaner, going into the back. Lou could hear her fishing about inside a drawer. 'Here, but make sure you return it or I'll be in trouble.'

'I'll be as quick as I can.' Lou raced back upstairs. Slowly, she turned the key in the lock. Come on!, she cursed, wiggling it hard. Then the door burst open. Lou held her breath. Thank goodness, no-one was inside.

She went to the window and looked out. David was a dozen yards down the opposite pavement, leaning against a lamppost. He saw her at the window and indiscreetly waved as well as thumbed up. Idiot! Lou moved quickly out of sight.

She looked around. Even though it was a bright summer's day it was gloomy in there. The room was messy and stank of cigarettes and stale sweat from unwashed clothes strewn across the floor. Two empty beer cans sat on the dresser beside a scrunched-up cigarette box and a pile of loose change. Not all the coins were English. Some looked strange with a harp on the back. Irish? The bed was unmade. A curled-up newspaper poked out from beneath the duvet. It was yesterday's *Sun*. As Lou picked it up, the remains of a half-eaten pizza slid out. The girl gaped in disgust. Slovenly pig!

Where should she look for clues? It was hard to know where to start. She yanked open the dresser's stiff top drawer. There were papers inside, old petrol receipts, a supermarket till receipt. She pushed her fingers to the back but there was nothing else. The second drawer would not open, so she wrenched it violently causing the whole dresser to shake, knocking the beer cans to the floor.

There was a spiral-bound notepad inside and a diary. It was a small, battered, leather-bound thing with such fine pages it was difficult to turn them. Lou cursed as she tried to find that day's date. It was blank anyway but there were entries for the following day, Saturday, and for Sunday.

She could not understand them. They looked like a series of jumbled up letters, possibly a code. She did not have time to figure it out and could not risk taking diary – if she did, the smuggler would be sure to realise someone was on to him.

Lou had a stroke of inspiration. She reached inside her

jacket pocket and took out her compact digital camera and set it to Macro mode for close-range photography. Flash, flash, flash! Within seconds, she had copied several pages of the diary. She turned to the front and noticed there were a few telephone numbers and took a picture of those.

Lou replaced the diary and turned to the notepad. As she opened it, footsteps could be heard on the stairs. She shoved the pad and diary back in the drawer and slammed it shut. Lou looked in alarm at the bedroom door, which was slowly opening. Someone was coming, it was too late to hide!

It was the cleaner. 'Are you finished up here love, I'll need that key back from you, else I'll be for it, she said. 'Bloomin' heck, your dad's a messy one ain't he?' said the woman, looking around her.

'He's not,' began Lou, about to say, scornfully, that the man lodging in that room was most definitely not her father. She checked herself just in time. 'He's not that good at being tidy,' she spluttered.

'Typical bloke, they're all the same, love, all the bloomin' same,' declared the cleaner.

'I know, where would they be without us women?' replied the twelve-year-old, confidently, handing back the key.

'You're right there, sweetheart, you're quite right,' said the cleaner, grinning with what few teeth she still had. 'You wanna meet my fella, waste of space he is.'

'You know, I'm going to take some pictures of this room to shame my dad!' said Lou.

She pointed the camera this way and that and took several, as the cleaner guffawed with laughter.

'Thanks for your help. I've got the sun tan lotion,' fibbed Lou, patting her pocket. 'I'm off to the beach now.' She handed over the key and vanished down the stairs, not wishing to remain in the hotel a moment longer.

She forced herself to walk calmly down the gravel

drive – running would look suspicious. David was still there, propping up the lamppost and looking bored. Lou jabbed him with a finger.

'Oi, you're supposed to be the sentry! Job done. We won't go back the way we've come, we'll go via the main beach. Come on, and I'll tell you what happened.'

She led him into the dunes, took out the camera and scrolled back through the pictures on its tiny digital screen. The sun was bright and it was difficult to see anything.

'So we're no further forward,' said David.

'Don't be daft,' came the sharp reply. 'We need to get these pictures downloaded to my dad's computer to view properly. I didn't get a chance to copy his notepad but with any luck there'll be something interesting on these diary pages.'

Lou stood up and gazed out to sea. From this angle, only the island with the lighthouse was visible. The bay was full of boats and the beach heaved with holidaymakers, milling about on the sand and paddling in the water.

Little did they know that in their midst was a gang of criminals not interested in enjoying a relaxing holiday, but seeking to flood the country with fake money. And what did they plan to spend it on? The thought made her shiver. Then, among the crowds, she spotted a familiar face. 'Oh look, David – there's Eifion, my old Welsh friend. Come and meet him!'

The pair ran to greet the elderly man who beamed with pleasure at seeing Lou. He was delighted to find that David also turned out to be an English youngster learning Welsh.

'This is a lovely place you've come to. *Y lle gorau yn y byd* – the best place in the world,' enthused Eifion, '*Pen Llyn*, the Lleyn peninsula. Wonderful scenery, wonderful coastline, and charming little beaches dotted here and there . . .'

'We're planning to explore the peninsula,' said David, 'and sail around the coast.'

'I'm sure Lou will take you, if you ask her nicely,' Eifion said, eyes sparkling like the sea.

'Eifion, do you know much about smugglers landing on beaches in this area?' blurted out David.

That was an indiscreet question and Lou shot him an angry look.

'Er, you know, tales from long ago of smugglers and shipwrecks and that sort of thing,' added David. 'There must be more to this place than farmland and fishermen.'

Eifion smiled, his sunburnt face crumpling into a hundred wrinkles. 'Oh there's far more to this place than farming and fishing, my young friend. These days that doesn't make local folk much money. It's you tourists we rely on now. In the past though, there were major industries here and mining too.'

That got David's attention. He was fascinated by mines. 'What sort of mines?' he asked.

'They used to extract manganese ore from the hillside of Nant Gadwen, above the beach at Porth Ysgo and at Rhiw. They worked it from the nineteenth century right through to the 1920s, I think it was. To this day, you can still see remnants of the old works, the ruined stone huts scattering the hillside and the winding gear, rusting away, and old spoil tips nearby,' replied Eifion.

'Are there still tunnels through the hillside, leading deep underground, where the miners used to work?' asked David.

'Yes indeed.' Eifion looked impressed at the boy's interest in his tales. 'If you go to Porth Ysgo, you can still see the tunnel entrances. In the old days, the manganese ore would be dug out with pickaxe and shovel, then transported along tramlines down the hillside to a jetty at Porth Ysgo. The ore would be loaded onto boats bound for factories where it was used to strengthen steel and make it more durable. I used to enjoy seeing those boats come in, they were a fine sight. The mines closed long ago, of course.' Eifion's eyes misted at the memory.

'Why did they close?'

'It's like everything, laddy, the manganese could be bought more cheaply elsewhere, from abroad I think, and a better quality, too. In the end there was no market for it. As for smugglers, there are many tales of their comings and goings along this coast over the centuries,' continued Eifion, leaning on his stick as he got into his stride. He would talk all day now, if the children let him.

'What sort of things were smuggled?'

'Brandy, rum, tobacco, tea, wine, candles, you name it. Anything which customs taxed through the roof, folk would try to bring in on ships, to the unguarded coves and creeks along the Lleyn peninsula,' said Eifion, staring fixedly out to sea. 'They'd sell the booty on for a good profit, too. If they were caught, mind you, they would be severely punished – locked up for years and some would even hang.'

David shivered but Lou had heard this tale numerous times before.

'Would they come to places like Whistling Sands – Porth Oer,' David wanted to know, earning another impatient glance from Lou.

'Oooh yes, Porth Oer, definitely, was among them. There's a cave there where they hid their loot. There were many other places, Porth Dinllaen, Bardsey, Nefyn . . .' Eifion's voice trailed off. 'Of course the smugglers have gone now. We won't see their like again, I doubt.'

'They're from another bygone age, aren't they Eifion?' chipped in Lou, anxious to cut the conversation short. 'Well, we really must go. Lovely to see you again.'

Eifion waved with his stick as the pair walked away.

'You really are a clot at times, David,' chided Lou as they strolled round the rocks beneath the yacht club to the bay the other side. From here, they could make it back to the caravan site without walking along the main road. 'This is a close-knit area. We must not let on to anyone what we know, not for now. It's secret. We must be careful. Don't even hint about modern-day smugglers even to people we trust, like Eifion.'

David's face fell a little, and he nodded.

'Well done anyway for your help this morning, and your bravery last night,' she added, more softly.

As they approached Lou's holiday cottage they parted. David returned to the caravan and Lou to her parents, eager for a chance to get on her father's laptop and download the pictures. She bounded up the rocks and along the steep path to the cottage.

'Hello mum,' she said cheerily as she walked into the kitchen. Her mother was making cups of coffee.

'Oh, have we got visitors?' asked Lou, counting three cups.

'I thought you were out for the day with your new friends,' snapped her mother. 'We don't need you in the way this morning.'

'Why, what's the matter, why are you in such a bad mood?' asked Lou, not that there was anything unusual in that.

Lou heard voices, one was her father's, the other she did not recognise.

'It's a man from the estate agent's,' Mrs Elliott explained. 'He's come round to value the property, see how much it's worth.'

'But why do you need to find that out?' asked Lou, her voice quavering a little.

'Because your dad's gonna sell up, that's why. Why do you think,' snarled her mother.

'Oh no, he can't sell!' pleaded Lou. 'I love it here, especially now I've met the others, we can't leave!'

'Oh but we can, my dear,' came the cold reply. 'Your

dad's not earning nearly enough to pay the bills. We can't afford it any more. He's not getting enough work in, idle so-and-so.'

'Well you're a fine one to talk, aren't you mum! When did you last do a day's work?' retorted Lou, tears in her eyes. 'You just slob about in front of the TV all day long.'

Lou realised she should not have said that but it was too late.

Her mother strode over to her, eyes blazing. She grabbed her daughter by the hair and shook her. 'Don't you *dare* talk to me like that. Don't you *dare!*'

'It's the truth and you know it,' replied Lou, her emerald eyes flashing with rage. 'You *are* a slob, keeled out on the sofa watching chat shows all the time and boozing and smoking. I don't know why my dad married you.'

Slap! Her mother's long, bony fingers connected hard with Lou's right cheek.

'You little madam!' she screeched. 'Clear off out of this house and don't come back. Go on, you heard me.'

'I'm going, don't worry. Tell dad I'm borrowing his laptop for a bit,' Lou said, spotting it on the sideboard and grabbing it.

'Hey, you come back with that,' shouted her mother, but Lou was away, fleeing down the path to the beach.

Lou pulled up, panting, and began to cry and Lou almost never cried. She sobbed in misery at the horrible row with her mother and the even more horrible prospect that their holiday cottage was to be sold. She hated to think that she wouldn't see Jack and the others again.

If that is the case, I'll run away, I'll live in my cave, vowed the youngster. She brushed her tears away and walked up the beach through the dunes to the caravan site, gripping the laptop bag tightly.

Lou made her way speedily and silently to her den and texted the others asking them to come as soon as possible. She filled her kettle and placed it on the camping stove.

As it boiled, she booted up the laptop and downloaded the pictures from her camera. She stored them in an obscurely named-folder which she hid on the desktop so her father would not find it.

Lou really needed the company of her new friends just then, and she couldn't wait to show them the pictures of her visit to the smuggler's hotel room.

CHAPTER THIRTEEN

A storm and some bad news

A STEAMING mug of tea in her hand, Lou stood at the cave entrance and looked out. Come on, you lot!, she thought to herself. More than half an hour had passed since she texted Jack. So far, he had not replied. Joe the crow landed and waddled up to her.

'You're getting fat,' she said, eyeing him fondly. 'You must be eating too much! Where have the others got to, Joe?'

The crow opened his beak and went 'clack'.

'Well that's a lot of help!'. Lou glanced at her watch. She sent Jack another text.

About ten minutes later, came his reply: 'Sorry for delay. Something's happened. Will be over ASAP.'

Her mobile beeped again. This time it was a text from her father. Lou opened it, puzzled, she didn't normally receive messages from her parents. He was apologising for not telling her they were selling the cottage, but money was now so tight they had no choice. A tear fell from Lou's eyes onto the screen of her phone. Reading this short, terse message from her father made things worse – so much more final. How cruel, now that she was having such fun at Abersoch with her new friends. No more seaside, no more sailing, no more den and no more Jack, David and Emily.

Lou looked up at the sky. The sun had retreated behind slate-grey clouds and the temperature was dropping. It was getting dark, although it was only mid-afternoon. Lou lit her paraffin lamp and its flame sent flickering shadows dancing up the cave wall. A whole hour had now passed. Lou wasn't the sort to mope but a very promising day was turning sour. She picked up her book. Reading might take her mind off things. Just then, Joe hopped into the cave entrance, lifted his little black head and clacked extra loudly, as if making an announcement. Suddenly, her friends appeared. At last!

'Where have you been?' she asked. 'I was worried, especially when I got your text. Are you in some sort of trouble?'

The others piled in and sat on the rugs.

'We're in danger, Lou,' said Jack. 'The smugglers – they know what caravan we're in.'

'Oh no!' she said, staring at him in horror. 'How come? I thought we agreed to be careful!'

'We thought we were being. Anyway, this morning, after you and David went off to the smuggler's hotel, Emily and I went for a walk on the beach with mum and dad and the dogs,' said Jack. 'We walked along the main road through the site, which we shouldn't have done, but I suppose we felt safe with our parents.'

'Ok, go on,' said Lou.

'Well, we had a long walk on the beach, throwing stones and sticks for the dogs,' continued Jack.

'Get on with it,' said Lou, irritated.

'On the way back, after we crossed the road to the site, we noticed two men hanging about in the car park. It was the smugglers, Mick and Griffo! Emily grabbed my arm and pointed at them and they saw her. They followed us through the site and back to our caravan. When we got your text earlier, they were at the side of the road, leaning against a telegraph pole, watching our caravan,' said Jack. 'In the end we decided to come to your den anyway, through the neighbours' back garden because from where they were standing they couldn't spot us. But we certainly couldn't have used the road or anything.'

'Why on earth did you brazenly walk back to your caravan with them trailing behind you in the first place?'

said Lou, staring at the three of them in dismay.

'We had no choice, Lou,' said Emily in a trembling voice. 'We were with mum and dad and we couldn't tell them anything. I suppose we felt safe with our parents and so we just let it happen.'

'You're fools. You should have thought on your feet, you should have done something,' said Lou. 'This is a nightmare! What are we going to do, you aren't safe! Looks like you'll have to go home It's too dangerous for you to remain at Abersoch now!'

'Don't say that,' said Emily, on the verge of tears. 'It's my fault for nudging Jack, I didn't mean to, I didn't mean them to spot us!'

'Look, I'm sorry I snapped at you,' said Lou, realising she was upsetting Emily. 'I'm a bit rattled too.'

She told them about the row with her mother and the text message from her father and how they planned to sell the cottage. 'So who knows? Looks like we could all be going home,' added Lou, gloomily.

As they talked, the sky darkened further, as if night were falling but it was only mid-afternoon. The clouds overhead had turned an ominous yellow-grey. The air was still and close. Lou recognised the signs.

'It's going to thunder and pour with rain,' she predict-ed. 'What a day this is turning out to be.'

She was right. The wind grew steadily stronger and began throwing itself around the woodland as if in a bad temper, making the trees groan and creak. Then the rain started. Huge drops one after another thumped down hard at the mouth of the cave forming puddles in the grass.

'Don't worry, we'll be nice and dry in here,' said Lou.

The children dug themselves deeper into their rugs, relieved that the woodland den was so cosy.

'The smugglers will get a good soaking, if they're still out there,' said Emily, making the others laugh. 'Oh Lou, what are we going to do?' Her cornflower eyes gazed at the older girl pleadingly.

'We'll think of something,' replied Lou, confidently. 'Jack, text your parents to say you're having tea with me tonight and won't be back till late. We'll lie low here this evening. You'll be safer than at the caravan. Oh and I have a few photographs to show you and an exciting story to tell, so cheer up, everyone.' Lou tapped the laptop and grinned.

She got in a round of hot chocolate while the computer booted up. The rain was bucketing now – they could do with a comfort drink. A flash of lightning far above the trees lit up the cave. A few seconds later came a loud rumble of thunder. Lou stuck her head out. The sky was almost black in places. The wind was blowing harder than ever. The tide must be in too, for the surf could be heard roaring high up the beach.

Not a good day to be out in a boat!, thought Jack.

Lou lit a few tealights and placed them on the stone shelf, filling the cave with a yellow glow. The others looked at her and felt secure. Lou Elliott was their unquestioned leader, with whom they felt they'd be ok, no matter what.

She sat down with them, cradling a mug of hot chocolate in her hands. They listened intently as she told them of the trip to Mick's hotel that morning, and how she'd tricked the cleaner into lending her a key to his room.

'And now for the slide show,' she said. She began to call up the pictures now stored on the laptop. 'Welcome, everybody, to your guided tour of a smuggler's hotel bedroom!'

The others laughed as they looked at the shots of Mick's messy room. 'Ugh' they all said in unison, at the close-up of the half-eaten pizza, which Lou just had to photograph.

'Now for the important ones. Most of the diary pages were blank,' she explained, 'but there were a few strange entries over the coming days like this one. I didn't have time to copy all that many.' She pulled up the picture of the diary entry for Saturday, the following day.

The children looked at it, puzzled. Lou zoomed in on the picture so the strange combination of letters written under that date could be seen clearly: P. UP WS – DEL YSG.

On the page for Sunday, was printed P.UP YSG. What could the letters mean?

'It's some sort of code,' suggested Jack. 'Each letter probably means something altogether different. So for instance, the letter P might represent a D perhaps.'

'Or perhaps not. How are we possibly going to break that?' said David, looking at Lou.

'I don't know,' she replied. 'I was hoping you might work it out, you're good with languages and spellings. Have a go, David.'

The others looked at him and the boy twiddled his now empty mug uncomfortably. 'Oh it's no good,' he said, after a few seconds. 'I don't have a clue, sorry.'

'Erm, perhaps it's not a code at all, perhaps it's an abbreviation,' said Emily timidly. 'It's just that there appears to be a dot after the letter P.'

Suddenly David gave a cry, making the others jump. 'Yes, Emily could be right! It may just be an abbreviation, not a code at all.'

'Can you read it?' said Jack, 'it doesn't make any sense to me.'

'P. UP,' read David. 'That could stand for "pick-up" and DEL could be delivery. WS could be Whistling Sands! So, there's a pick-up from Whistling Sands and a delivery to YSG tomorrow and then the following day, a pick-up from YSG, perhaps moving the same goods on somewhere else.'

'That's good, David,' said Lou, impressed. 'You're doing fantastically. Now, what will YSG mean?'

They looked at him expectantly. He stared hard at the letters, willing them to make sense but this time he was stumped.

Eventually, he said: 'If WS stands for Whistling Sands, YSG is also likely to be initials of some kind. I certainly don't think there's any word beginning YSG. Oh hang on, yes there is – ysgol – it's the Welsh for school. They can't mean a school, surely?' He paused. 'Or maybe, Y, S and G are initials. The letter Y in Welsh means "the", so it could even be a Welsh name: "The" followed by two words beginning with an S and a G.'

'Ok,' said Lou. 'That's a pretty good start. From this, it looks like the smugglers will bring in cargo to Whistling Sands tomorrow by boat, then deliver it to YSG, whatever that is.'

'I wonder what the cargo will be,' said Emily.

'More superdollars at a guess,' said Jack. 'Someone will presumably meet the boat as it comes ashore with a van of some kind. They'll load up and drive off to YSG. My guess is that YSG must be a storage warehouse, possibly a large garage or outbuilding. It might even be at a school or located close to one, which would explain the initials. Or as David says, it might stand for a Welsh name beginning with "The". 'Trouble is, the entries give no clue what time anything will happen.'

'They will probably come and go after nightfall, although we can't assume that,' said Lou. 'They could come anytime from the morning onwards. Anyway, we must now decide what to do.'

She thought for a moment then turned to the others, looking serious. 'I'm afraid I really do think it is too dangerous for you to remain at the caravan at the moment, now that the smugglers know which one you're staying at. But I've got an idea,' Lou added, as the others looked at her in horror. 'If the smugglers are going to Whistling Sands sometime tomorrow – why don't we go back there and camp? It will get us out of trouble here, and give us a chance to spy on them!

'Our going there won't cross their minds, she pointed out. 'We won't camp on the main beach. We'll go along the coast a bit where there are tiny coves, but still near enough to keep watch out to sea. You can see for miles from the coastal path along the headland above. It won't matter what time they turn up because we'll be waiting for them.'

The others looked at each other. It was a marvellous, exciting idea, to go off with Lou camping, on the trail of smugglers! Emily felt uneasy, but she felt even less keen on staying behind with Griffo and Mick on the prowl.

'Why don't you go back now,' advised Lou, 'and ask your parents' permission. If they say yes we can leave early in the morning before anyone's up. You know something, I think the rain has eased off.'

In fact, the rain had disappeared completely along with the wind. A couple of stars could even be seen in the late evening sky. Lou flicked on her torch and led the others carefully along the woodland path to the caravan site. She wished them good night and returned to her den.

Careful to make no noise, Jack, David and Emily gently opened the caravan door. Their parents were on the sofa, watching TV. Mr and Mrs Johnson had been getting anxious with the storm raging, but were impressed that their rather reserved children had been out having fun with Lou. They not only agreed to let them camp with her but offered to give them a lift first thing. That would be better than cycling from the caravan site and risk being seen.

The Johnson youngsters experienced difficulty sleeping that night. The caravan no longer seemed the safe refuge it once did. And although they were planning to flee the smugglers they were also seeking them out.

Lou's mind swirled with many thoughts as she burrowed deep into her sleeping bag beneath a rug in her cave. She hadn't fancied returning to the cottage. Her parents weren't the sort to worry about where she'd got to, after all. But she worried about them, and the money problems they faced, and their lovely little holiday home.

Her mind filled with pictures of the dollars now stuffed into a bag only an arms-length away from her at the back of the cave. Money beyond her wildest dreams! If only they could use it to save her dad from going bust and prevent him selling the cottage. If only . . .

She told herself to get a grip and stop being so stupid, then fell fast asleep.

CHAPTER FOURTEEN

Scare in the night

THAT night Jack dreamt he was running through very soft sand and after him came two burly men with fat bellies shouting at him and waving their arms. His legs gave way beneath him and they jumped on him, pinning him to the ground.

He awoke, his heart racing. After a few seconds he realised that he wasn't on a beach at all but in bed at the caravan and the only thing on top of him was his duvet cover. David was snoring gently in the bed alongside him. Jack sighed with relief and pushed his head back into his pillow. But then he heard a strange noise.

Tap! Tap! Tap!

Jack ignored it, certain it was just his dream starting up again. But the noise came a second time. Jack sat bolt upright.

Tap! Tap! Tap!

It sounded as if someone or something was knocking on the bedroom window! It was slightly ajar as the night was warm. Jack swallowed hard, reached through the curtains, grabbed the window handle, pulled it shut and locked it. Slowly, he parted the curtains and looked out. Nothing was there, or was that a figure slipping away in the shadows?

Jack got back into bed and told himself it was just his over-active imagination. He had been having some vivid dreams recently, that was all. Reassured it was nothing untoward, he fell back to sleep.

By 5.30am, daylight was seeping round the curtains. Jack awoke and stretched. If he opened the curtains just a fraction there would probably be enough light to read his book by without disturbing David. He glanced towards the window.

That's when he saw the note. A folded-up piece of paper was lying on the carpet below. He picked it up, smoothed it out and read it. He turned pale.

'Crikey,' he said under his breath. 'It's a note from the smugglers!'

Written in capital letters in black ballpoint pen, were the following chilling, misspelt words:

WE NO WHO YOU ARE. WE NO YOU HAVE OUR CASE. RETURN IT UNTOUCHED OR YOU WILL BE IN BIG TRUBLE. PUT CASE UNDER CARAVAN, BEHIND CENTRAL WEEL, SAME SIDE AS YOUR BEDROOM. WE WILL PICK IT UP TOMORROW NITE. IF YOU DONT YOU BE SORRY

Jack's heart pounded. He stared at the note in horror. So it wasn't a dream! Someone had come in the night, noticed the window was open and dropped that note through. David was stirring and Jack shoved it into the pocket of his pyjama trousers, out of sight.

'Are you awake, David? If so, let's get moving so we can leave as soon as possible,' said Jack.

Before long, their parents were up too, while Emily continued to sleep soundly. The boys busied themselves packing for their camping expedition. Jack zipped the note into his jacket pocket, ready to show Lou later. At 7.30am came a sharp tapping on the door. Jack had a mug of hot tea in his hand and spilled it over himself, jumping in fright.

'Oh really, Jack, what's the matter with you? You're a bag of nerves this morning,' said his mum.

'Come on in, Lou,' she said, opening the door. 'You don't need to knock you know, I'm starting to think of you as one of the family.'

Lou smiled warmly at Mrs Johnson. It was a nice thing to say.

'Give me your rucksack, Lou, and I'll put it in the car,' said Mr Johnson. 'Where's your bike – oh yes, on the patio, I'll put that in too.'

Mrs Johnson handed Lou a cuppa. The girl looked at the others. 'Good night's sleep?' she asked.

'Yes thanks,' replied Emily, 'although I had some funny dreams.'

'Not too bad,' said David.

'Not great,' admitted Jack, yawning.

'Now, do you want a cooked breakfast before we set off?' asked their mum.

'We'll get off now, thanks,' Jack said. 'We can cook some brekkie when we get there.'

After his experience in the night, he wanted to leave as soon as possible. It looked like the good weather had returned after the previous day's storm. A pale blue sky with a couple of cotton wool clouds greeted them as they got into the car. The children looked around nervously as they drove off through the site and turned right towards Abersoch. They were relieved to see nothing suspicious.

Mr Johnson signalled right again and turned up the steep hill towards Mynytho. As he did so, a silver car pulled out of the nearby boat garage. Was it following? The children glanced at each other. Before long, it turned off towards Llangian. The road was now reassuringly empty. No-one was behind nor in front. They sped along easily, soon approaching Aberdaron and the turning for Whistling Sands.

It was hot and sunny when they arrived at the grass car park on the cliff-top overlooking Whistling Sands.

'Now, where will you camp?' said Mr Johnson, striding towards the road down to the beach. 'Not that way,' said

Lou. 'We're going to pitch our tent on the grass to the left of the main beach.'

The others followed as Lou took them along a sandy path which led from the car park through a thicket of small trees. The path twisted then fell away steeply down some steps and out onto the wide, grassy coastal path overlooking the cliffs.

'Look at that wonderful view,' exclaimed Emily. 'What a simply vast ocean.'

It certainly was stunning. From here, you could see for miles along the coastline both east and west and a huge distance out to sea. Jack, David and Emily had never seen the sea look so enormous.

'This will make a great look-out point,' said David, earning himself a stare from Lou.

Mr and Mrs Johnson helped the children pitch the tents on the flat stretch of grass Lou indicated, then went back to get the rest of their things, including bikes.

'I think your parents deserve a cup of tea,' said Lou with a grin, lighting the camping stove.

They all sat down on a rug together enjoying a brew and a few biscuits. Lou rather liked having Mr and Mrs Johnson there. She was so used to parents who didn't bother with her, she appreciated their company. Their mugs drained, Paul and Liz Johnson bid the children a somewhat reluctant farewell. Lou guessed they would rather have liked to join them.

Emily watched as her parents disappeared. She and the others were now on their own at Whistling Sands! It made her feel a little strange.

She said, in a small voice, 'we will be ok won't we?'

'Of course,' said Lou, giving her a hug. 'We will be fine, believe me. Isn't this a wonderful spot!'

Their tents were pitched on a square of grass invisible both from the coastal path above and vessels out at sea. They were just round the corner from the main beach where all the holidaymakers would go. It was an ideal spot.

'Come on,' said Lou. 'Let me show you something.'

They scrambled down the bank which gave way to a rocky slope, beyond which was a cove, mainly covered in shingle but with a small stretch of sand.

'A hidden cove!' cried Jack, as he slithered down to it. 'I never even knew it existed!'

'Hardly anyone does,' said Lou. 'All the tourists go to the main beach. From here, we can easily look out to sea and if smuggling boats come ashore on the main beach near to the little access road, they will need to pass very close to this cove. No-one will spot us in the dark, and there are loads of boulders to hide behind if we needed to.'

'You're assuming the boat comes in from over there,' said David, pointing west. 'What if it sails from the opposite direction?'

'If it's coming from Ireland as we believe, it will sail in from the west, and that will bring it close to this cove,' said Lou. 'Also, from here it's much easier to get back onto the coastal path along the cliff-top where we can see for miles and look down on the beach road. Later on, we will have to take turns on look-out.'

Jack was bursting with excitement at the prospect, the scare in the night forgotten for now under a warm midday sun. On look-out! That would be fun! He glanced around the cove. It was only small and bounded on either side by huge seaweed-draped rocks smothered in barnacles and bright orange lichen. He helped Lou light the barbecue. They were all starving having skipped their customary cooked breakfast.

'You see those boulders over there,' said Lou, pointing. 'We could do a driftwood fire behind them later and sit round it, if it gets cold. It won't be seen out to sea.'

'I'll start collecting some wood,' said David. He went

off to the far side of the cove where driftwood had been thrown ashore by the tide. It was smooth and bleached almost white by the sun, and bone dry.

Emily clambered back up the slope to fetch their tin plates and cutlery from the tent. Jack looked out to sea. Unlike in the bay at Abersoch, there were no speed boats or noisy jet bikes zipping about. They had this secret cove entirely to themselves. It was peaceful here and he felt thankful they had got away when they did.

Alone with Lou for a moment, Jack decided it was a good time to tell her about the note pushed through the window in the night, without the others overhearing. As he pondered what to say, the incoming tide lapped round his bare feet and he gasped at the cold water.

'Mummy's boy,' said Lou, teasingly, as she had on the day they first met.

She put her fingers to her lips as Jack was about to protest. 'I don't think that any more you know,' she said, smiling.

Jack glanced at Lou, at her long, dark hair rippling in the sea breeze. She looked fearless and striking. He remained somewhat wary of her, as he had been during their first encounter but nonetheless was thrilled to have someone like her as a friend. He didn't know anyone quite like Lou. His trust in her was absolute while at the same time he felt some trepidation about where their adventure might lead. Did danger lie ahead? He did not have her courage.

Lou saw the affection in his eyes but also sensed his unease.

'Don't worry, Jack, it will be ok you know, it's all going to be fine,' she said.

'Lou,' Jack said, stammering as he fished the note out of his pocket, 'there's something I must tell you. I didn't like to mention it in front of the others. Last night in bed I heard a tap at the bedroom window. Someone was trying to frighten us. Then they pushed this through.' He handed her the scrawled note from his pocket.

Her eyes opened wide with shock. 'Why did you not let me know before? You should have alerted me. These people are clearly trying to scare us off. What a horrible thing to do. Do the others know about this?'

'No. Nobody knows. I didn't dare tell mum and dad and I didn't want to scare David and Emily,' replied Jack. 'Fortunately, David slept soundly through the whole thing.'

'Thank goodness we're out of Abersoch,' said Lou.

'But are we safe here?' asked Jack.

'I don't know,' the girl replied. 'Certainly safer than at Abersoch. But we must be really careful. This just shows how determined they are to get the case back. In a way though, this note is a good sign. These people may be criminals but they're also idiots, Jack. They're clearly on the bottom rung of the ladder. Look how dreadful their handwriting is and full of spelling mistakes. I bet they haven't got a brain cell between them. On the other hand,' continued Lou, staring out to sea, 'the people that will come tonight will be higher up the chain, sharper and more intelligent, and possibly more dangerous. Not a word to the others about this, ok?'

Jack nodded.

At that moment there came a loud thud as David hurled a pile of driftwood onto the sand next to them. 'Loads and loads of wood, all shapes and sizes!' he said. 'I've also brought some seaweed to throw on to make the fire crackle and pop.'

'I've got the plates,' cried Emily, as she scrambled down the bank.

'Great,' said Lou. 'Come on, let's get the food cooking, I'm hungry.'

Mindful of their important task that evening, Lou rummaged in her rucksack, checking her digital camera and binoculars were safely stored. David and Jack got the driftwood fire going. They started off with smallish twigs which hissed and crackled as flames from a firelighter licked around them. After that they threw on some larger pieces. There was something very satisfying and reassuring about getting a good fire going.

'This will provide useful warmth later on when the sun goes down,' said Jack. 'I don't suppose we'll get much sleep tonight.'

CHAPTER FIFTEEN

Sun goes down on Whistling Sands

'OK everyone, food's ready,' called Lou.

Jack sat on a flat rock and munched his burger contentedly. They were in their very own secluded cove with not an adult in sight. What could be better! He gazed out to sea almost in a trance, enjoying the sight of the waves crashing against the rocks.

The children enjoyed their barbecue. There was something indescribably special about eating hot food at the seaside in the salt-tanged fresh air washed down with a mug of steaming tea. It was a warm, sunny day, tempered by a sea breeze. They sprawled out on the small envelope of soft sand, feeling very relaxed. Lou got her book out while the others snoozed, lulled to sleep by the gentle ebb and flow of the tide, gurgling and crackling its way across the seaweed and shingle. Eventually, the peace was broken when a large seagull mistook David's motionless tummy for a rock and landed on it. The boy let out a girlish shriek, sending the bird soaring into the air in fright.

'If you scream like that when the smugglers come we'll be done for,' scolded Lou, as the others laughed. She stretched and yawned. 'Come on everybody, it's time we got moving and made a few plans.'

Emily roused herself too and put the tin kettle to boil on the charcoal. It was late afternoon now and the sun was beginning to drop lower in the western sky. She pulled out jumpers from the rucksack. They might need them before long. Jack and David stoked up their driftwood fire and threw more sticks on.

Later, when the holidaymakers had gone from the main

beach, they would keep watch out to sea. Jack, David and Lou – not Emily because she was too young – would take it in turns to clamber up the slope to the coastal path on sentry duty.

'Remember how easily noise travels at the coast and particularly at night,' Lou warned the others. 'David – please – no more shrieking. If another seagull lands on you, don't say anything, or if a crab crawls over you for that matter.'

'Ooh, crabs,' exclaimed David. 'I hope not.'

Everybody laughed, and he shot his once familiar scowl at them all. He still didn't much like being teased.

'Listen,' said Lou, earnestly, 'the point is we must be totally silent tonight. We must not be seen or heard. If they spot us or hear our voices they will instantly suspect something and will either clear off or come after us.'

Emily glanced at her watch, it was now 8.30pm. She decided to make some sandwiches while it was still light. The girl was a little jumpy now, but determined not to show it. She was sad not to be required for watch duty, but relieved too. Anyway, she could be useful tending the fire and making sure the others were supplied with food and drink.

The children nibbled the sandwiches she made them as the shadows lengthened, and the light began to fade. Lou had packed a watchman's rucksack containing binoculars, her digital camera, a small but powerful torch, bars of chocolate, and a small notepad and pencil.

'Right. It's 9pm and I'm going to take the first watch,' she announced. 'Jack – you're to take over in two hours' time, ok?'

Jack nodded and in a flash, Lou was gone, bounding up the hillside with the rucksack on her back. A look of apprehension crossed the faces of the others as she disappeared.

'Come on, David, let's get that fire going again,' Jack said cheerily.

Before long, it roared upwards. There was certainly no shortage of driftwood, blown in from the sea through the winter months. They felt better as the flames shot into the darkening blue sky and warm air filled the cove.

Meanwhile, on the cliff-top above was a young girl who feared nothing, least of all being alone in the dark. Lou was at her sharpest when by herself. She wanted to make full use of the waning light while she could. She looked out to sea through her binoculars. The water remained calm although its colours were darkening, becoming a deeper blue, in places purple. The sun was dipping fast, streaking the sky around with a stunning mixture of red and pink and sending forth a final finger of gold across the water.

Satisfied there was no danger yet out to sea, Lou darted along the coastal path to observe the main beach. It had been full of tourists earlier but now just a handful remained. As the sun finally dropped below the horizon they got to their feet, shook the sand off their towels and began to leave.

Lou observed them closely. The coastal path turned inland above the steep beach road, giving a good bird's eye view of comings and goings to Whistling Sands. As the stragglers, stiff from too much sunbathing, plodded across the sand and up the road, Lou shadowed from the path above, imagining they were smugglers. She could see and hear them most of the way back to the car park. They, on the other hand, had no inkling they were being watched from behind thick shrubs and reeds covering the hillside to their right.

The girl turned and gazed back down the beach. Whistling Sands looked different with no-one about, it was no longer so cheerful. In the twilight, the sand was a yellowish grey rather than gold and inviting as before. All around her, tiny moths fluttered among the bushes. There was scarcely a sound, save for the occasional wail of a sea bird – or was it David – Lou grinned to herself, and a distant murmur of cattle and sheep.

A while later, she looked back out to sea. The water was now purple-black, and the bright white finger of a full moon rippled across it, riding high in a starless sky. Still she saw nothing.

Any normal boat would show lights but, of course, it was no normal boat they waited for. It was nearly 11pm and time for Jack to take over. Lou returned to the cliff-top above their cove and listened intently. Silence. Then she stiffened slightly, was that a light from below? Lou fled from the path and dived for cover.

CHAPTER SIXTEEN

Night watch

'LOU!' called out a familiar voice. 'Where are you?'
'Keep quiet you idiot,' hissed Lou, 'and switch that torch off! It could easily be seen out to sea!'

'I'm sorry, I never thought,' stammered Jack, again forgetting to whisper.

'Shut up! Or I'll get Emily to take over in a minute.'

Jack felt crestfallen. He yearned for approval in Lou's eyes and wanted in some daft way to be a hero that night. Now, he had messed up before he'd even taken over the watch.

Lou handed him the rucksack and binoculars. 'Check the coast first, scan from left to right, and keep glancing behind you. Then walk the path above the beach road looking out for vehicles using it. Listen carefully for any suspicious noise on land or at sea, particularly the sound of an engine. If you see or hear anything, come and get me. Oh and there's chocolate in the bag if you get hungry.'

With that, Lou slid away without saying anything further and returned to the cove. Jack was cross with himself and disappointed. He had hoped she would stay a while and watch the coast with him together.

But Lou wished to check David and Emily were ok and not too scared. They were snuggled by the fire behind the large rock, their faces glowing pink in the light of the flames. They brightened up when she appeared out of the shadows.

'It's so nice to see you, Lou,' whispered Emily. 'Is anything happening up there?'

'No,' Lou whispered back. 'Not yet.'

For two long hours Jack kept watch above. The moon-light made it possible to see for some distance. He felt excited, elated and scared rolled into one.

The sea remained calm with only a light breeze to ruffle its surface. Occasionally the boy thought he saw some-thing, only to realise that it was surf from a breaking wave, caught in the moonlight. Sometimes he heard a strange oinking – a seal or a dolphin perhaps? At one point, an engine rumbled a long way away. The sound came no nearer. As his eyes adjusted to the dark, he could make out the contours of the rocks below, the inky water, the grey box-shape of the beach café; the gorse and shrubs around him. He listened hard for the slightest disturbance to that warm summer night. There was nothing.

At 1pm sharp came David, scrambling up for his turn of duty. Jack returned to the cove where the fire was burning down, a little disappointed.

'I hope we can trust your brother to watch properly,' whispered Lou, doubtfully. She feared he might panic in the dark and scream or something.

In fact, David wasn't scared at all, just sleepy.

There's clearly nothing happening, he thought to him-self after he'd scanned the coast and peered down towards the beach road. He sat on the rug and yawned. He tried hard to listen for anything suspicious but all he could hear was the gentle lap-lap of waves washing the rocks below.

A breeze got up a little. It was warm and gently per-fumed with the spiced-vanilla scent of gorse flowers. It stroked his face and caressed his nostrils. David felt pleased with himself as he burrowed deeper into his coat. It was, after all, thanks to his bravery trailing Mick back to his hotel that they were here now, patrolling the coast.

I would once have been petrified up here in the dead of night, now look at me, he told himself, admiringly. And, unlike Jack, he hadn't flashed a torch up and down and got into trouble with Lou.

The binoculars weighed heavily in his hand. He let them slip onto the rug. Then he allowed his head to loll back into the hood of his coat which felt like a soft, comfortable pillow. Nothing was happening. It wouldn't hurt to lie down and shut his eyes for a short while. Just a minute or two, no longer . . .

In the cove, Jack and Emily huddled together for warmth by the fire. It was getting colder now. They were feeling sleepy. Lou, however, was wide awake and pacing about. Suddenly she leapt with cat-like skill onto a rock. Was anything happening out to sea? She could see and hear nothing but a feeling of unease came over her.

It was just after 2am. David had been on guard duty for an hour now, had he noticed anything? Lou left the others and pulled herself noiselessly up onto the slope to find him. She whispered his name but there was no reply. Then she heard a strange noise, what sounded like . . . snoring!, followed by a short sigh.

Just visible in the moonlight, curled up on the rug like a dog, was David. Lou was furious. She felt like shouting the hillside down. She put her hand over his mouth to stifle any cry and gave him a sharp prod. 'Wake up you clot. I knew I couldn't trust you.'

Now it was David's turn to feel small. Lou pulled him up by his coat and gave him a good shake.

'I'm sorry, Lou, really. I don't know what happened, I must have sort of dropped off,' whimpered David. 'I was just really tired.'

'You're a disgrace,' sneered Lou. 'I can't trust you – get back to the cove now and send Jack up – you can stay down there and look after Emily.'

David did as he was told, too ashamed and sleepy to argue.

Shortly afterwards Lou heard something, not seawards

but inland. The distinct murmur of an engine, she was sure of it. She did not have time to wait for Jack to appear. She ran along the coastal path, through the gate and then took the path above the road. She stopped halfway where she had the best view and hid in the bushes.

A small stretch of the road was visible in the moonlight, lit up like the stage of a theatre. She could hear only the breeze which had lulled David to sleep. Perhaps it had been a car passing close by on its way to Aberdaron. Yet the sense of danger did not leave her.

She remained where she was, silent and alert, watching and waiting. She glanced towards the bay, at the black incoming tide topped with ghostly white spray. Then, in the corner of her eye, she thought she saw something at the top of the beach road. It looked like a greyish-white lump of some kind.

Get a grip!, she told herself, fearing her imagination was playing tricks.

But something resembling a huge, unwrapped pack of lard was slowly floating silently downwards. Lou watched, numb with amazement and fear. Was this a ghost, was this what ghosts looked like? As the greyish lump passed beneath the moonlight, she saw what looked like two eyes as big as lamps!

They *were* lamps. The ghost was actually a white van, rolling gently down the hill to the beach with its engine and headlights switched off. It approached the seashore café and turned into the nearby parking bay. The smugglers had arrived! It must be them!

Oh, how exciting this would have been if the sun still shone; if the others were alongside her and if scented barbecue smoke rose into the air. Instead, Lou was alone in the dark, with only the enemy for company. For a fleeting moment, she was afraid. Cold panic rose inside her.

But only for a moment. Then her eyes narrowed as she looked upon the van and her fear was supplanted by a sense of determination and purpose. She sprang up and sped back to the cliff-top. By now Jack was there, wondering what had become of her.

'Jack, they're here, they have brought a van down to the beach!' she gasped into his ear, clutching him. 'Now, you're going to have to be brave. I want you to go to the beach and watch for the boat to come in.'

Lou fumbled for a moment in her bag and brought out something which glimmered in the moonlight. She fiddled with it then handed it to Jack. 'It's a video camera – set to night vision. It will record in darkness. Get yourself to where you can see the shore, and let it film.'

'Where did you get this wonderful camera from, is it yours?' he asked.

'Shush and do as I say.' Lou was in no mood to explain she'd borrowed it without permission from her father.

'What about David and Emily?' asked Jack.

'Don't worry about them, they will be fine where they are. There's no point us all running about this hillside. I'm going to try and get a look at that van and see if I can read the number plate,' said Lou.

'I'm scared,' said Jack.

Lou grabbed him by both arms and gave him a gentle shake. 'This is your chance to be a hero, Jack. I'll be so proud of you if you get these men on film. Listen out for any clue where tonight's delivery is being taken. Remember – we think it's somewhere called Y S G – do your best to overhear them.'

With some misgivings, she sped back up the hillside.

In the cove, Emily gave David a gentle shake to wake him. 'Where's Lou?'

'She's probably gone to help Jack keep watch,' said David, yawning.

'I'm getting cold,' said Emily. 'The fire's nearly out, could we put some more wood on it?'

'I don't see why not, I don't think anyone would see it. Anyhow, there has been no sign of those smugglers.'

David got to his feet. He was stiff and sore from sitting for too long on hard rocks. The moon had disappeared although there was still some natural light. He glanced out to sea. He rubbed his eyes, still half asleep. Whatever was that?

Some kind of shape, like a giant, pale blue kite, was hovering just above the water. He rubbed his eyes again, and told himself not to imagine things that weren't there. Yet the 'kite' was coming closer. David shivered. The moon suddenly appeared from behind a cloud and glared down on the bay. The 'kite' was in fact a boat's sail. A boat with no lights, voyaging slowly and silently towards Whistling Sands beach. David stared, transfixed. A hand reached out to his shoulder and he jumped in fright.

'It's only me, silly, what's the matter?' said Emily.

'Look,' he whispered. 'There's a boat coming in,'

Emily clutched his arm. 'David, they're here. It's them. It must be!'

'We must find the others and warn them. They would be looking for lights and the boat isn't showing any. Come on, Emily.'

Had it not been so dark, David would have seen the look of fright on her face. She was trembling and un-steady. She grabbed her brother by the arm and clung to him.

'We'll be ok,' said David in his most reassuring voice, although he too was scared and anxious to find the others.

They picked their way gingerly to the rear of the cove and scrambled up to the coastal path. At the top they crouched low, fearing they might be seen. There was no sign of Jack or Lou.

'Oh David,' said Emily. 'What could have happened?

Where have they gone? Have they been captured?'

'I don't know, I hope not,' he replied. 'I'll go and look for them, you go to the tent and try and get some sleep.'

'David please don't leave me,' begged Emily, clutching him tightly. 'You can't leave me alone, not in the middle of the night, with them here.'

'Then you'll have to come with me,' he said.

'No!' she whimpered. Her body shook uncontrollably.

David put his arm round his sister. 'Ok, come on, let's both go to the tent. I can't risk leaving you like this. I'll stay with you; Jack and Lou will have to look out for each other.'

With that David half carried Emily to the tent and got her safely inside. He knew he had no choice, but he felt terrible. The others might need him yet he could not go to their aid. He prayed that no harm would come to them.

CHAPTER SEVENTEEN

Lou takes a risk

JACK picked his way in the dark along the path to the shore. Huge rocks ringed this side of the beach like giant teeth and were easy to hide behind. He got as close as he dared and put the view-finder of the video camera to his eyes. The camera was in night-vision mode and recording as if it was daylight. He nestled his elbows into a crevice to prevent it shaking and pointed it seawards.

There, a few dozen yards away, a boat was coming in! Its sails had been furled. He could see men sitting inside and two other men on the beach waiting for them. The smugglers! And here he was recording them, capturing their activities on camera. It was the most exhilarating, terrifying thing he had ever done.

His right hand nervously moved to the top of the camera, feeling for the zoom button in the dark. He found it and pressed.

Suddenly everything looked very close indeed, as if he could reach out and touch them. The men on the beach waded into the water. One grabbed a rope from the prow of the boat and dragged it onto the sand. He could see it more clearly now. It was a medium-sized yacht with a cabin and a powerful outboard engine mounted on the stern.

One man disappeared into the cabin then popped up again, holding something. Jack could not make out exactly what. It looked like baggage of some kind – carrying more superdollars, perhaps?

Jack began trembling again and the camera shook. He told himself to stay calm. He needed to keep a cool head and keep recording. After the shame of his brother being caught napping on duty, it was important he did not also mess things up. He was frightened, but a subconscious desire to impress Lou spurred him on. Lou had entrusted him with this important task and he was determined not to let her down. This was his chance to shine in her eyes.

Right then, Lou was not concerned with how Jack was getting on. She had enough to worry about. She guessed the men in the van would head to the shore to meet the incoming boat. She would have a few crucial minutes to take a look at their van while no-one was around.

She wanted to read its number plate and note it down. It was risky. She couldn't have asked anyone else to attempt this. She was desperate to discover where they planned to go next. Where was Y S G, what did those initials stand for? You Should Guess, said Lou to herself, wryly.

Back on the hilltop path overlooking the road, she could see the white roof of the van below. The slope down to it was covered in shrubs and reeds which would provide good cover.

She listened intently and could hear no sound from the vehicle. As quietly as she could she began to descend. She slithered and slid, cursing as she occasionally stepped on twigs in the undergrowth which snapped under her feet. 'Yuck!' she exclaimed in disgust, discovering that in places it was boggy, and her feet squelched up to her ankles in mud.

Eventually, she reached the bottom. From the light of the moon there appeared to be no-one in the cab. Luckily, the front of the van could not be seen from the beach. She crouched, listening hard for the slightest sound. Lou slunk almost on all fours to the front wheels, whipped out her tiny torch and shone it at where the number plate should be.

She struggled to see it because, close up, the 'white' van was filthy, caked in mud and grime. The number plate was too dirty to be read by torchlight. The initial letter looked like an S but she could read no more. She felt in her pocket for a hanky and was about to spit into her hand to start cleaning it when it occurred to her that it might take several minutes – time she didn't have. What's more, they might notice their number plate was clean and become suspicious.

She dared not go round the rear of the vehicle because from that angle she could easily be seen from the shore. Anyway, the rear number plate would be as bad. She was perplexed.

Then she had an idea. The tax disc on the windscreen would have the registration number recorded on it. Lou jumped onto the jutting out front wheel, sprang onto the bonnet, shone the torch onto the disc and sure enough! It was printed clearly in black ink – SD04VHP. Lou jumped back down again, memorising the number and sunk into the bushes. She whipped out her pencil and paper and wrote it down, hands trembling.

That task had not proved too difficult, so perhaps she should jump up again and flash her torch inside the cab through the windscreen? That might yield valuable clues. Lou inched out again and leapt back onto the bonnet.

She was about to switch on her torch when she heard the squeak of the 'whistling' sand underfoot. The van shook. To her horror, she saw through the windscreen the rear doors opening. The men had returned! Lou froze, too terrified to leap off. Through the driver's window she saw a man's shoulder. He was about to get into the cab.

Instantly, the girl bounded onto the top of the van, pulling herself onto the roof rack. She spread-eagled herself, preying she hadn't been seen. The vehicle shook again as the cab door opened and a man got into the driver's seat. He hadn't seen her. But now what was she to do?

Lou heard thuds as one of the others pushed something

into the rear of the van. So, there were smugglers loading up the back and another sitting in the front seat. She was trapped! Why had she gone back to the van? Why? She'd got what she needed. How totally, completely stupid!

She rested a few seconds, trying to regain her composure. There was no point panicking or getting angry with herself. The van would not move for a while yet. Getting off via the bonnet was no longer an option. There might be a chance to slide off the sides or the back if she timed it right.

Meanwhile, no-one would see her so long as she remained flat. To and fro the smugglers came, hurling baggage of some kind into the rear. She counted the number of seconds it took them to walk to the boat and return.

About thirty – enough for her to jump down and escape. Gingerly, she edged to the side and looked down. No-one was there, only, what was that? A tiny orange light glowed a few yards away. It was one of the gang, sitting on the sand, enjoying a cigarette. Blow! He would easily be able to see her.

There was nothing for it. She would have to wait for them all to get inside and, as they were about to get going, she would jump. They wouldn't hear above the noise of the engine. The men returned with another bag.

'Oi, finish that fag and start helping, you lazy so-and-so,' one of them shouted, presumably at the smoker. The orange glow disappeared. He must have finished his cigarette but in the darkness, Lou couldn't be sure exactly where he was. It was too much of a risk to leap off just yet.

'Ok we're done,' said another with a distinct Irish accent a few minutes later. 'Get this straight round to Isgo, ok? The truck's coming for the lot tomorrow night.'

The passenger door opened and one of the men got in.

'Be seein' ya!' shouted the Irish voice again.

Of course, groaned Lou. At least two of the gang had arrived by boat and would return the same way. They were evidently going to stand there until the van pulled away, to see off their mates, robbing her of her chance to jump.

Suddenly the vehicle began to judder and give a low growl. The engine had started – it was about to go, with Lou clinging to the roof!

CHAPTER EIGHTEEN

A breakthrough

FORTUNATELY, the lumbering and now heavily-laden van could only crawl up the steep road from the beach. Lou held on tight to the roof rack. As it neared the top of the slope it laboured and came virtually to a stop while its driver clumsily changed to a lower gear. But in a minute or two, it would turn onto the flat, public road and speed away. Lou had to seize this chance. She jumped like a gazelle into the soft undergrowth at the side of the road preying she didn't drop into anything thorny.

She landed perfectly, bending her knees and falling forwards to soften the impact. She rested a few seconds to get her breath back. She was bruised, scratched and shaken up but otherwise ok. Lou reached into her pocket, grabbed her paper and pencil and wrote down the words she had overheard – *Isgo, tomorrow night*.

The van drove on, picking up speed as it reached the flat, public road. She had got off just in time. Lou gasped in relief. She waited until she could no longer hear the sound of the engine, then straightened up, got back onto the road and walked into the empty grass car park. She would take the route through the trees back down to the coastal path. How had Jack got on, she wondered? He better not have lost that video camera. That would take some explaining back home!

She weaved her way between the rocks on the shore, deep in thought about these strange people who came and went mysteriously in the dead of night. She had never come across anything like this before. She hoped no harm had come to Jack, where was he?

'Jack,' she called, softly, 'are you ok, where are you?'

'Lou, is that you,' came a voice from behind a crop of rocks a few feet away.

'No, I'm one of the smugglers, and I've just caught you.' She slipped down to greet him, and gave him a hug. 'I'm so glad you're ok,' she said.

'I was a bit scared at first, but then I was fine,' replied Jack, stoutly

'Of course you were scared, so was I,' said Lou. 'But we're ok, that's the main thing. Is the camera all right, did you manage to film anything?'

'I filmed loads and it's recorded fine – after the smugglers left a few minutes ago I've been playing some of it back.' Jack pressed Play to show Lou some of the footage he had recorded.

'You're wonderful.' Lou gave his arm a squeeze. 'Did you manage to hear anything they said?'

Jack shook his head. 'I heard their voices but couldn't catch their words.'

'Well you never know what we might see and hear when we play the tape back properly. We better find the others. I hope they're ok. Hold my hand, so you don't slip.'

They walked carefully back along the path to the tent. It was darker now than before because the moon had disappeared behind heavy cloud. They still didn't dare put their torches on. Lou unzipped the tent and they crawled in. She switched her torch on.

'It's ok, the smugglers have gone,' she said. 'Are you both all right?'

David and Emily looked anxious. Emily's eyes were tired and puffy.

'We didn't know where you were,' said David. 'We've been worried. I was going to come after you but I couldn't leave Emily, she wouldn't let me.'

'I'm sorry, I was so scared, I just had to stay here and I needed David with me, I'm sorry,' repeated Emily, who looked about to cry.

'Don't worry,' replied Lou, 'no-one's cross with you. David did the right thing to stay with you. Everything's fine. Jack and I had an exciting time, there's loads to tell. Look, why don't we get back down to our driftwood fire, get the kettle going and we'll tell you all about it?'

It was half-past three in the morning but no-one felt like sleeping. They picked their way carefully down the steep slope to the cove. They could dimly see ahead despite the absence of moonlight. The sea no longer looked black but dark grey. Another day was dawning.

The fire hadn't quite gone out, embers still glowed red beneath charred logs. Jack and David hurled an armful of driftwood on. Before long it blazed up and began to warm them, and in each pair of cold hands was a tin mug of steaming tea. Lou scrabbled around in a side pocket of her watchman's rucksack and dug out some chocolate which she broke into four pieces and handed out. They smiled weakly but cheerfully at each other.

In a hushed voice Lou and Jack told the others their stories. David and Emily listened in amazement to Lou's terrifying account of her ride on top of the smugglers' van. And they were astonished to hear how Jack had hidden behind rocks and brazenly filmed the boat coming ashore. He brought out the video camera and played back what he'd recorded.

'Look, there's Griffo and Mick!' exclaimed David. 'I'd recognise those bellies anywhere.'

Jack said: 'They must have been driving the van, and the others were in the boat.'

'Where do we go from here?' asked Emily. 'They've gone off in the van and ok we now know its registration number but we don't have a clue where they've gone.' She rather cheered up at the thought.

'We do have a clue,' said Lou. 'They said something about delivering to Isgo – and a truck picking up the cases tomorrow night. Who knows where that will be, it could be anywhere in the whole country. I've never heard of Isgo before.'

'Ok,' said David, thinking carefully, hoping he could say something useful as he hadn't contributed much overnight. 'Like we said yesterday, these deliveries are coming in by sea on small boats, being picked up by a van and then, probably, stored somewhere locally, ready for one big pick-up. Remember what we found out on the internet, the superdollars are destined for cities like Birmingham. But what's puzzling is that, according to the diary, the cargo was being delivered to YSG, whatever that is. Now we think it's Isgo – are there two storage places?'

'Are you sure you're pronouncing it properly, Lou?' said Emily. 'I mean, if it's local it's likely to be a Welsh name and . . .'

'Listen, you! I can speak Welsh, I know how to pronounce things. I was only repeating what they said after all,' retorted Lou.

'So, maybe *they* weren't pronouncing it properly,' added Emily.

David looked at her then rose from the rock he was sitting on in triumph. 'I've got it!' he said. 'Well done, Emily!'

'Oh thanks!' Emily was pleased she'd helped although she wasn't sure how.

'Lou, the smugglers you overheard talking about Isgo, did they sound like Griffo and Mick, or did they have Irish accents?' asked David.

'They had Irish accents, it was the smugglers who came in by boat. They were giving orders to Griffo and Mick, I remember quite clearly,' said Lou.

'Ok, so when they said Isgo – they may well have meant Ysgo, which should be pronounced *"uh-sgo"* in Welsh,' said David. 'So the letters YSG in the diary entries would simply be short for Ysgo!'

'But is there anywhere round here called Ysgo?' asked Jack.

'Yes!' said Lou, understanding David's train of thought. 'Porth Ysgo, a nearby beach round the coast from here, the other side of Aberdaron. I can't believe I didn't think of it before.'

'But why pick up stuff off one beach, only to drive it round to another?' reasoned Jack. 'If they want to store their cargo at Porth Ysgo, surely they could sail it direct to Porth Ysgo, why come here first, then drive it round?'

David reflected on this for a moment. 'Well, there must be a reason, because that seems to be what they're doing.'

'Whistling Sands is much bigger and easier to navigate to in the dark,' pointed out Lou. 'The bay at Porth Ysgo is surrounded by huge boulders, some of which lie just below the surface. I wouldn't much like to sail to and from it at night and I know the coast round there well. Whistling Sands has an access road leading right down to the beach. As we saw tonight, stuff comes in by boat and can be put straight into the back of a waiting van and whisked away. At Porth Ysgo you'd have to lug it across a beach covered in stones and shingle, up a steep flight of wooden stairs, then along a grass path running beside a brook, up to the road.'

'So, Porth Ysgo isn't going to be where they'd want to store the cargo, either,' objected Jack.

'It must be, and we need to find out why,' said David, determined to make up for his failings overnight. Whistling Sands is where they prefer to bring stuff in, but Porth Ysgo must be a better place to store it. There must be somewhere secret perhaps, somewhere no-one goes, where they hide their deliveries until the big truck comes for the whole lot. And that's what's going to happen tomorrow night, according to the diary, which as it is now Sunday morning, will actually be tonight!'

'Somewhere secret, somewhere no-one goes,' repeated the boy, frowning as he thought hard. 'Well of course. The tunnels in the hillside above Porth Ysgo!'

Jack and Emily stared at him blankly, not having heard Eifion's story, but Lou turned to him in excitement.

'The tunnels lead to big caverns from the days when miners dug for manganese back in the 19th century and early 20th. Eifion told Lou and me about them when we met him on the beach, continued David. 'Perhaps they now have another use – as a storage warehouse for smugglers!'

The children looked at each other with bright faces tinged with weariness. Their next task must be to head to Porth Ysgo in search of the smugglers' hidey-hole. They had to get there that day, because sometime that night the cargo would be picked up and all evidence of their illegal activities would be gone.

'I'm so tired,' said Emily. 'I'm fit to drop.'

'We're all fit to drop,' replied Lou. 'We don't need to go straightaway. Let's go back to the tent and have a few hours' sleep. We must aim to get off by 11am because it'll be about half an hour to cycle there and we'll need to stop in Aberdaron. We must get to Porth Ysgo by 2pm at the latest so we have the afternoon to search before it gets dark.'

At that moment, a chill breeze blew in from a choppy sea, and the children felt a few drops of rain. That settled it. After such a dramatic night, they were in no mood to get soaking wet. They returned to the tent, curled up and within seconds were fast asleep.

They didn't hear the wind whistling through the tent pegs, nor the pitter patter of heavy rainfall on canvas. If any smugglers had returned as the clocked ticked round from 4.30am towards midday, they would not have been troubled by anyone spying on them or clambering over their van. For now, the young sentries of Whistling Sands were in a very different place.

In their dreams, of course, they were still on duty. David, snoring lightly, was back watching the cliff-top imagining he was wide awake and hadn't dozed off after all. Jack pictured himself seizing the smugglers' boat and zooming off in it. Emily's mind filled with images of the smugglers discovering her and Jack hiding in the tent. Lou's was turning, not to the night before but the one to come and she felt a sense of foreboding that they were to be captured. She awoke and gazed fearfully at the tent roof, realising with relief that it was only a dream.

The children did not stir until nearly 1pm. They had slept for more than eight hours. Lou was cross with herself when she finally came round. Chances are they wouldn't now get to Porth Ysgo before 3pm. She roused the others. 'Come on, we've overslept. We're not going to have much time to search if we don't get a move on.'

They left the tent and some of their belongings behind, unable to carry much on their bikes, taking just small rucksacks. Back on the road, Lou pointed to the spot where she leapt off the van. They turned and stared down the steep road leading to Whistling Sands. The sea was once again a deep blue under a warm sun. It was rougher today, they noticed.

'There's a boat out to sea,' said Emily. 'I wonder if . . .'

'They're lobster fishermen,' interrupted Lou. 'I know them. Look, you can see them pulling up their baskets. Come on, we must go.'

The children stopped in Aberdaron on the way to buy sandwiches, realising they were hungry. They loved the seaside village and Emily begged to go to the quaint café Gegin Fach for a coffee and some cake.

'Emily, please take this seriously,' snapped Lou. 'Those men are coming tonight – which could mean anytime from 7pm onwards. If we leave it much longer it will be too dangerous to go looking.' Lou suspected

Emily was dragging her heels for precisely that reason. She added, more gently, 'we'll be ok, you know. One final push that's all.'

But she could see the troubled look in Emily's eyes and guessed that she was close to giving up on their mission. 'Ok, come on, let's go and get a coffee and a cake, said Lou, reluctantly.

The children left their bikes outside the centurics-old Gegin Fach, its thick stone walls gleaming white in the sunshine. Emily felt better with a slice of coffee and walnut cake in front of her and a hot, milky coffee. Then she meekly enquired whether it would be best to just tell the police what they knew, leave it up to them and return to Abersoch.

'We could go straight to the police,' said Lou, her mouth full of cake, 'but they wouldn't necessarily believe a bunch of young children. They certainly aren't going to spend hours looking down tunnels at Porth Ysgo based on our guesswork. Anyway this is our adventure, not the police's. When we've found the smugglers' hide-out we'll call them and they can come and see for themselves. What do you boys think?' she added.

Jack and David agreed with Lou, of course.

Emily nodded. 'What a story we're going to have to tell one day!' she said, popping the last bit of cake in her mouth.

'Thanks for being so nice with Emily,' whispered Jack to Lou as they left the café and mounted their bikes.

'That's ok,' replied Lou.

Except that a glance at her watch told her it wasn't ok. They had lost yet more valuable time which could only make their task more dangerous.

CHAPTER NINETEEN

Astonishing find!

AS they struggled up the hill towards Rhiw, approaching Porth Ysgo, Lou pulled over.

'Hang on a minute,' she said. 'This is the one place around here I can get a signal on my mobile. I'll check if I've had any messages.'

The others stopped, glad for a rest. Jack switched his phone on, too. A text came through from mum and dad hoping they were having an enjoyable time. On Lou's phone was a text from her father. Her heart sank. He wouldn't just be saying hello. It must be something important.

'Oh no,' she said, under her breath. 'Jack, look at this!'

Her parents had received an offer for the cottage – a poor one but they were desperate for the money and it would allow them a quick sale. They were to sign a contract on Tuesday and the new owners wanted to move in by the end of the week.

Her parents needed the place cleared straightaway, and could Lou please return that day. To her friends' horror, Lou burst into tears. They had never seen her in this state before.

Jack put his arm round her. He wanted to tell her things would be ok but this was simply awful.

'We can't let this happen, Lou. Not now we've all become friends. You mean so much to us,' he said.

'You all mean a lot to me too,' she replied, giving his hand a squeeze. 'But I can't see how we can stop it. Anyway, one thing's for sure,' she said, smiling grimly and wiping her eyes, 'I'm certainly not going home tonight. They can forget that! Come on, let's get off to

Porth Ysgo while we've still got time.'

'Here at last!' said Lou, when they turned down the lane leading to Porth Ysgo. It was nearly 4pm. They were much later than intended. Lou was troubled. She had been ever since her strange dream. Was it a warning? Then her father's text. It seemed a bad omen. They now had very little time to find the smugglers' hideout before nightfall.

The children lifted their bikes through the rusty kissing gate leading to the long path down the hillside to the shingle beach of Porth Ysgo. There was, in fact, a choice of paths. One followed the brook which burbled its way along the foot of the valley towards the shore. But there were other routes higher up the hillside.

They walked alongside the brook. After a while Lou stopped and pointed. 'Look up there!' A hole disappeared into the hill. 'That's a tunnel into the old mine workings, there are a number round here. Some are more visible than others. And, over there – ruins of stone huts. They were built by the miners.'

'Oh look at that,' said Emily, in amazement. 'A rusty old mine wheel.'

'Do you see that huge dark pile of loose stones and rubble? That's a spoil heap from the mines,' said Lou. 'I'll go and check that tunnel out.'

She pulled out her torch and shone it inside as she approached. Slightly nervous, Lou entered the tunnel and began to follow it. It was narrow with a low roof, damp underfoot and the air was stale. Lou shone the torch at the muddy floor looking for clues anyone had been this way recently. There were no footprints, no marks, discarded litter, nothing. But there was a coin.

She picked it up and shone the torch at it. It said 'One Penny' – but was much larger than the pennies Lou was used to. It must be old money unused for decades, perhaps dropped by a miner long ago. A few yards further, a tangle of rusting wire blocked her path. The girl turned back, blinking in the bright daylight as she emerged.

'I don't think that's the one. No-one's been in there for ages. I did find some money though, but I don't think anyone would call it super,' she smiled, showing them the coin she'd found.

The children moved on, examining other holes, crevices and fissures in the rock. When they reached the clifftop overlooking Porth Ysgo beach they turned back, this time taking the path half-way up the hillside. Then they checked out the higher path. Their investigation yielded a couple more holes and passageways, but they were no more promising than the first. Time ticked by and before they knew it, it was gone six o'clock. Tired and hungry, they stopped for a break. They had only cola and two bags of crisps between them and wished they'd saved some of the sandwiches bought in Aberdaron earlier, but it was better than nothing.

'It's like looking for a needle in a haystack,' moaned David, despondently.

Surprisingly, Emily had perked up and was now eager to keep going. 'We're looking into all the obvious places, the ones anyone could see if they walked past, but maybe the passageway they chose is hidden from view. Also, it's more likely to be at the top of the hill than the bottom because they want to move things quickly.'

'I think you're right,' said Lou, frowning as she concentrated. 'Perhaps there are holes into the hillside which are no longer easy to find, that have been covered over. Also, remember this, those men have made several recent journeys here, including last night. Therefore, we ought to look for clues like trampled grass and bracken and maybe discarded cigarette butts and things like that. Let's go back to the gate near the road and retrace our steps and this time, look for odd-looking paths which appear to lead nowhere.'

They hadn't got far when Lou pointed. 'Over there, the other side of the brook. Do you see how thick the bracken is? Well, doesn't it look like it's been sort of pushed aside a bit? Some of the stalks are bent and broken.'

Unhelpfully, right at that moment, a sheep emerged from that very spot.

'Oh well, that answers that,' said David, giving up again.

'Shush David,' said Lou impatiently. 'It doesn't answer anything. There's some kind of funny gap in that bracken and I don't believe it was made by a sheep. If you look carefully, isn't there a rock face behind it? Come on, let's go and have a look.'

'I can't see any cigarette ends,' remarked David.

'I didn't say we'd see any cigarette ends,' replied Lou, irritated, 'but that is the sort of thing we might see which would give us a clue. Aah, a clue like this! Look under that gorse bush – beer cans and a couple of beer bottles.'

'Oh aren't people awful dropping litter like this,' said Emily, sounding like her mum.

'This might be what we're after,' said Lou. 'Somebody has definitely been this way and recently. Look, there's a footprint in some dried mud. People have trampled through this bracken and now we've found a pile of old beer cans and bottles. In fact, they're not particularly old at all.' She jabbed at one of the bottles with her foot and chipped it out of the undergrowth.

It was an empty bottle of French lager but the label was clean as if it hadn't lain there long. Lou picked it up. On the back was printed 'best before end' and the date underneath was April the following year – a full twelve months away.

'These have been dumped recently,' said Lou.

'Anyone could have chucked them down here,' protested David.

'Only why would they?' asked Jack, who understood

Lou's interest. 'We've walked a slightly-trodden path through thick bracken which seems to lead nowhere. Why would anyone come drinking here?'

Lou pushed through the bracken towards the rock face and the others followed. 'There! That's why!'

In front of them was an opening cut into the rock. It was similar to the others, only this was impossible to see from the main path. The children looked at each other. Lou pulled out her torch again and headed for the hole.

'I'm coming, too. If this is the place, it's too dangerous for you to go in there alone,' said Jack, trying to sound braver than he felt.

'And me,' said David, spurred on by his natural interest in mines – and a determination not to be outdone by Jack.

'Well, I'm not staying out here by myself,' said Emily.

Lou smiled at the thought of the bumbling brothers protecting her. More likely the other way round! 'Let's all go into the tunnel then. If we keep together, we'll be fine. I'll lead the way.'

A hole, barely big enough for the children to stand upright in, had been cut into the rock. The air was musty but good enough to breathe. The walls and floor were dry. At first they could only walk in single file, Lou in front with her torch on and David at the rear with Emily. Then the tunnel widened, opening into a small cavern. Something was on the ground ahead – a crumbling axe.

'It must have been left by a miner,' said David, fascinated. 'Imagine how long it's lain there.'

'Perhaps we're the first people to come here for a century or more,' mused Jack.

'Or perhaps not,' replied Lou, sharply, shining the torch back and forth. 'That's not been there for a century, has it?' She pointed to a piece of metal on the floor. She picked it up. 'My dad does a lot of DIY – especially now he hasn't got so much work on. He has loads of these, they're shelf brackets.'

'Why would your dad come down here?' asked Emily, who could be very clever one minute and a bit thick the next.

'I'm not even going to answer that,' retorted Lou, scornfully. 'So who, apart from my dad that is, comes here with shelving brackets? Who's been putting up shelves and where are they?' She flicked the torch round the cavern.

'Look,' said Jack. 'The passageway continues over there. Why don't we go that way?'

'There may be several passages. We mustn't get lost,' she replied, her voice echoing into the distance. 'We could easily lose our sense of direction.'

She threw the shelving bracket onto the tunnel floor to mark their way out. The passage turned right then opened into another cavern, much bigger than the first. The children gaped when Lou shone her torch upwards.

'Wow, this is like an underground banquet hall,' exclaimed David.

'You can see why some people love going potholing,' remarked Jack, in awe, 'you can go deep underground and find the most amazingly vast caves, far bigger than this one.'

'We're not on a potholing expedition, we're here for a reason,' cut in Lou, impatiently, shining her torch rapidly in all directions. 'We are here to see if we can find, if we can find . . .'

Her voice trailed off as the torch illuminated a wide metal frame containing several rows of shelves towering above their heads and running all the way down one side of the cavern. The children stared in disbelief. The shelves were crammed with suitcases, briefcases, rucksacks, sports bags – baggage of all shapes and sizes.

'It's like some sort of underground outdoor shop, what on earth is all this doing down here?' asked Jack.

Lou yanked one of the rucksacks to the ground. 'Let's

take a look inside one.'

There was nothing in the main part, but in a side pocket she touched what felt like a plastic bag. Lou pulled it out and tore open the packaging. They had seen this remarkable sight before: bundle after bundle of bank notes – American hundred dollar notes, just like the ones they had found in the briefcase!

There were thirty wads, each appearing to contain fifty one-hundred dollar bank notes – the same amount as before. Jack pulled down an ordinary-looking sports bag which he unzipped. He slid his fingers under the lining at the bottom. Sure enough, out came a package containing bundles of superdollars tied with elastic bands. David grabbed another and yet more wads tumbled out.

'There must be around fifty bags and cases on these shelves,' said Jack. 'If each one contains a hundred and fifty thousand pounds of superdollars, how much would that be?'

David tapped the sums into the calculator on his mobile. 'Seven-and-a-half million dollars, multiplied by nought point six, makes four-and-a-half million pounds,' he replied, matter of factly.

'FOUR-AND-A-HALF MILLION!' repeated Emily, amazed, her voice echoing through the mine. 'Ooh let me open a bag too,' she said, not wishing to miss out, turning to one on a lower shelf.

Lou was about to stop her, conscious of the time, but checked herself. Emily should be allowed to share this moment, too, especially since it was she who had found the original hidden package in the briefcase from the island. Emily unzipped a bag at random. It too, appeared empty but when she pushed her delicate fingers along the bottom, she felt the bulge of a parcel. She pulled it out and it was crammed with bundles of superdollars. She extracted one and held it up, proudly.

'Right,' said Lou. 'We've done fantastically well but

we must get out of here. We've already been far too long.' She shone the torch at her watch and tutted. 'It's gone nine o'clock.'

'But look at the mess, hadn't we better tidy up first, or the smugglers will realise someone is on to them if they get here before the police,' pointed out Emily.

'That's true,' said Lou, cursing inwardly at yet another delay. 'Come on then, shove the money back in the bags and push them back on the shelves, as quick as you can. We don't want to be caught here. I'll keep one bundle.' She stuffed it in her pocket. 'It might be useful if the police don't believe us.'

Suddenly, Lou, whose hearing was razor sharp, sprang to her feet. She snapped her torch off.

'Listen!' she whispered. 'I can hear footsteps coming down the tunnel. We must hide!'

CHAPTER TWENTY

Disaster strikes

THEY dashed to the end of the shelves, next to the rock walls and cowered in the shadows. Lou left the others and ran to the back of the cavern, where the tunnel continued deeper into the mine. Everywhere was utterly black. She was blind in the darkness. She reached out with her hands until they touched rough, cold rock. She pressed against the wall desperately seeking out the tunnel. Did she have time, just for a second, to flick her torch back on?

The voices were getting nearer. They were rough and harsh and sounded familiar. Griffo and Mick! The men walked into the cavern and the beam of powerful torches swept around. For a second, they lit up the passageway she was trying to find. But she had no cover, the men only had to look in her direction and they'd spot her.

'Right Mick, is everything ready to roll?' asked Griffo.

'Everything's fine, Griffo. All sorted,' said Mick. 'It's all here, we're only missing that one case those kids found. I reckon we'll get away with that. We'll have to say it was lost overboard or something.'

'You're an idiot,' said Griffo. 'You better hope we do get away with it.'

'Stop worrying will you,' said Mick. 'Look at that – ain't it bloomin' marvellous?'

He shone his torch along the shelves, admiringly.

'Hang on a minute,' growled Griffo. 'What's that down there?' He pointed to the ground.

The children's blood froze. They could guess.

'It's a bundle of notes. What is this doing lying loose on the floor?'

The children trembled in fright and cursed themselves for their carelessness.

'I er, I don't know Griffo,' said Mick, sounding nervous. 'It must've got dropped somehow.'

'I find that very odd. We better search the place!' demanded Griffo, swinging his torch up and down, his face appearing to glow with anger in the flickering torchlight. His powerful beam was about to turn in Lou's direction. She would be spotted instantly. She grabbed a loose rock and lobbed it over the men's heads towards the passageway they had just walked down. It clattered noisily behind them. They whirled round.

'Who's there!' shouted Griffo and Mick.

While their backs were turned, Lou got to her feet and fled towards the opposite tunnel, praying that her memory wouldn't play tricks on her. She found it, and crawled a short way along, her heart thumping. She was now mercifully out of sight but close enough to hear what was going on.

'Whoever is hiding in this place, come out now or I'll shoot,' rapped the cruel voice of Griffo, echoing menacingly round the cavern. 'Give yourselves up now.'

Mick began walking along the shelves, shining his torch up and down and across the floor. Jack, David, and Emily huddled together, their backs pressed against the wall; their hearts thumping. They could only hope against hope that his bright torch would miss them.

It didn't. They blinked and screwed up their eyes as a cylinder of blinding light encircled them.

'Get up!' Mick's harsh voice echoed around the cavern.

The three children slowly got to their feet, clutching each other for support.

'Griffo, just look what I've found – another bunch of infuriating kids.'

Mick pushed them into the centre of the cavern to face his boss.

'What are you doing here?' demanded Griffo, slipping a gun back into his pocket. 'This is private property and no place for children.'

'I'm really sorry,' spluttered Jack. 'We were just exploring, that's all. We're on holiday near here.'

'Where are your parents and where are you staying?'

Jack hesitated. He didn't want to be caught out lying but it looked like the pair didn't recognise them from their encounter on the caravan site. After all, it had been hot and sunny and they had worn sunglasses and caps. So much the better if he didn't make the connection.

'Answer the question.'

'We're staying in the Pwllheli area,' replied Jack, it was half-true – Abersoch was near Pwllheli, after all. 'We cycled to Porth Ysgo to look around the old mine-workings. Our parents aren't here, they let us come by ourselves. We love potholing in underground caves and passageways. When we saw these shelves full of sports bags we thought maybe this was a potholing club. Then we found that bundle of dollars on the floor. We didn't touch it, of course, because it's not ours. Maybe it's been lost by an American potholer?'

'Yeah and maybe you need dropping down a pothole from a great height, you cheeky brat,' said Griffo. 'My guess is that you took this money from one of the bags. Didn't you? How come you knew how to find it? Well?'

The men stared angrily at the children who merely stood there quaking. None of them replied.

Griffo and Mick turned their backs on the youngsters and talked in low voices.

'They're just a bunch of stupid, nosy kids trying to be explorers. I reckon we let 'em go,' said Mick.

'There's something weird about them,' said Griffo. 'How come they knew how to find the hidden cash? Could they be the same kids as . . .'

At that moment came a clatter. David had tripped over

the shelf bracket dropped by Lou in the tunnel marking the way out. The children were trying to escape. The men sprang on them in seconds and hauled them back into the cavern, then hurled them to the ground. Jack's elbow jarred as it connected with the cold stone floor.

'Don't think you're going anywhere. Potholing!' Griffo said, with a sneer. 'You're not potholing, you've come here spying, haven't you? That's why we found you cowering in a heap against the far wall. Why would you act so scared – wouldn't you expect us to be potholers as well? And what's more, I've a nasty feeling we've met you lot before. Haven't we?'

No answer.

'Well this time you're going nowhere,' snarled Griffo. 'We're going to tie you up until we've finished here. Then we'll decide what to do with you.'

Mick took some rope from a bag and roughly grabbed first Jack then David and bound their hands and feet. The men ignored the boys' protests to leave Emily alone and trussed her up too.

Lou was listening in horror. She ached to return and help but she was no match for two heavy, powerful men. Could she sneak into the cave unnoticed and get down the tunnel to the exit? Gingerly, she poked her head round and peered into the cavern.

She saw her friends being roughly tied up by Mick. Anger welled up inside her but she suppressed it. She couldn't prevent him – she had to focus on not getting tied up herself. The men didn't know that she was still free. That was her big advantage.

Griffo began hauling bags from the shelves and piling them in the passageway.

'Come on, Mick, how long does it take to tie up those kids,' he bawled. 'Get on with it and help me shift this stuff, the others are coming at eleven.'

So, their mates were arriving in an hour and a half. They would clear the place and escape and their efforts to stop them would have failed. More to the point, what would happen to Jack, David and Emily? What if they were taken away or harmed? Lou couldn't bear to think about it. She had to get out somehow and wreck the men's plans.

There was only one option and it was dangerous and unpleasant – to take the passageway deep below ground and hope it led to another exit somewhere. She pondered long and hard what Eifion had told her. The mine wasn't huge, nor did it run particularly deep.

In the days when it was a working mine, the manganese ore was collected in carriages running along tramlines. The tramlines crossed the production floor and came out the other side, halfway up the cliff-face overlooking the shore at Porth Ysgo. They then ran directly onto a specially-built jetty built on stanchions leading out into the sea. Boats would dock at the jetty and take away the ore. Lou could picture the scene from Eifion's old black and white photos. If she located those tramlines she could follow them until they eventually brought her out of the mine on the seaward side. They might have been ripped out, of course, or rusted away. Or the tunnel might have collapsed in places.

Any number of hazards might lie in wait but she had to give it a try. Lou switched on her torch and began walking. She stumbled along. Even though she was not quite five feet tall, the tunnel roof was so low in places she had to bend double. She pitied the miners who came this way all those years ago, particularly the taller ones. Dotted about were relics from those bygone times. Rusting pickaxes and helmets, even oil lanterns lay scattered, untouched and unseen for decades. What was that over there? An old knife! It must have belonged to a miner. Lou stooped and picked it up. Its blade, though corroded, was still strong. She pushed it inside her rucksack.

The tunnel split into two and the fork to her right appeared to slope downwards slightly. Perhaps that way was more likely to lead out onto the hillside. She followed it, shining the torch in front of her feet, examining the ground below. The air grew colder. The passageway widened. Lou was glad of the chance to straighten up. She flicked her torch around. She was in a huge underground room, possibly the heart of the mine. Piles of stones lay on the floor along with several rusting tools.

Her torch alighted on three metal boxes seemingly placed one after the other. Rail carriages? Yes, they were on wheels. Underneath were two parallel lines of corroded metal heading for the tunnel on the far side. Tramlines! Lou's spirits rose. She began to follow them, shining the torch along the metal strips which gave a dull gleam.

She strode forward eagerly – too eagerly. A coil of ancient cable lay unseen in front of her. It looped around one of her feet, yanking it from under her. She crashed to the ground, her torch flying from her hand as it smacked into the floor. The bulb shattered.

Lou's world turned black.

CHAPTER TWENTY-ONE

Time is running out

LOU pulled herself up and began to crawl forwards on all fours, her bruised fingers grasping for the tracks. She was now surrounded by total darkness. Those tramlines were her only guide. On no account must she turn round or she would become totally disorientated.

For a while, she made good progress. Then, ouch! Lou's head banged into something hard. She reached out to it – a rough metal box. It must be an old carriage. She staggered round it and continued. She crept along like some sort of insect. Her hands and knees were becoming tired and sore. Lou began to feel barely alive, as if she was floating through a void of complete emptiness.

She kept going, shuffling forwards, blistered hands grabbing desperately at the two lines of metal beneath her. She began to weaken; her limbs were shrieking with pain. She had to stop for a moment to rest.

Reluctantly, she leant forwards again, her hands on the tramlines, and restarted her crawl. And then the tramlines disappeared. They'd gone! Her hands flailed across the hard ground from side to side but nothing was there. She could feel them behind her, but not in front. Her lifeline had been taken from her.

Her heart thumped in her chest. A sense of panic swept over her. She was lost in a pitch-black underground maze. She bowed her face into her raw, swollen hands and sobbed.

After a few seconds she dried her eyes and swallowed hard, determined to put her despair to one side and keep going. I'm in a tunnel, she told herself. If I can touch the walls and the roof, I've still got a chance of finding my

way out. It must lead somewhere. Careful not to change
direction, she pulled herself painfully to her feet. She
raised her arm but was unable to touch the roof. She
stretched both arms out wide on either side of her, but
could not feel the walls either.

'Now I really am done for,' she whispered to herself.

Lou stood stock-still, entirely at a loss to know what to
do for the best. It occurred to her that she was starting to
see and hear things. A strange whooshing sound roared
through her ears. Somewhere at the top of her eyes was a
greyish blob. Was she losing touch with reality and going
mad?

That noise was terrifying yet strangely familiar. She
glanced up again at the blob hovering high up in her
vision. Suddenly, it turned into a dazzling white disc,
shining like a silver coin high above her. It was the *moon*,
sailing out from behind a cloud. Instantly, she recognised
the whooshing sound – the sea. There it was, in front of
her, dark grey, flecked with white, ceaselessly hurling
itself against the rocks below.

'I must be out of the tunnel!' she cried. 'I can see
again!'

The man in the moon, should he exist, would at that
moment have beheld a young girl smiling gratefully up at
him. She breathed in and out deeply. The sea air was
delightfully fresh and fragrant after the stale, oppressive
atmosphere of the cramped tunnel.

But what now? She looked about her. The tramlines
had brought her out, as expected, half-way up the cliff at
the point where they would once have run straight onto
the purpose-built jetty. It was an enormous relief to have
escaped from the mine, but how would she now escape
from the side of a cliff?

She faced an unappealing choice: scramble down to the
shore, or up to the hilltop with only moonlight to see by.
Lou thought hard. The shore directly below was just

round the corner from the main Porth Ysgo beach. Sturdy wooden steps led from the beach up to the cliff-top and from there, she could follow the brook back to the front of the mine.

But Lou knew this coastline well. She didn't fancy the idea of scrambling downwards. The lower part of the cliff was very steep. She might easily lose her footing. Even assuming she got to the bottom in one piece, she would then face having to clamber over huge boulders and rocks covered with treacherous green slime which she wouldn't see in the poor light. It was too great a risk, especially since her limbs were so sore and bruised.

Going up wouldn't be much fun either. She would face a stiff climb up a cliff-face strewn with gorse bushes, heather, shrubs and bare, stony patches, and the risk of falling onto the rocks below. But it wasn't quite so sheer and when she got to the top it ought to be an easier, more direct route back to the mine entrance.

Lou pointed her wristwatch into the moonlight. It was a quarter past ten. Griffo and Mick's mates were due to arrive at 11pm. She had just 45 minutes.

I'll go up, she decided. She glanced nervously sky-wards. She depended on lunar light. Was the moon about to disappear behind another cloud? There was the odd wisp floating around but apart from that it looked clear. Good!

Lou gazed at the cliff above. It was near vertical in places, with large stones jutting out from the badly-eroded clay surface. She swallowed hard and began to climb, grabbing thick tufts of grass to propel herself higher and finding firm footholds where she could. She winced as her fingers plunged into a spiky gorse bush that she mistook for grass.

She scrambled round it then over a bare patch, using rocky outcrops as a staircase. She tried not to look down as she climbed higher, lest it scare her. She fixed her gaze upwards at the ridge above, a dark silhouette beneath a twinkling line of stars.

A cloud, which Lou hadn't spotted, cruised slowly in front of the moon and blotted it out. The hillside turned from grey to near black. Lou had to wait patiently for it to move on, her feet pressed against a ledge. Come on, cloud! The ledge felt like it was starting to give way beneath her feet, or was it her imagination? She was right! The flattish protruding stone she was resting on fell, clattering down to the boulders beneath her. Her foothold gone, Lou started to slither down the bare cliff-face, which seemed to crumble away from her.

Grab something, anything! She thrashed out in panic. The man in the moon must have been on her side. His pale white face shone down again, lighting up the exposed root of a heather bush. Lou grasped it, praying it would take her weight. It did so – just – groaning horribly above the roar of the sea.

A shower of loose soil and stones pattered onto the rocks below. Lou swallowed hard, the root was holding, but her arms felt like they were being torn from her body. Somehow she found the strength to wrench herself up, plunging deeply into the heather above.

It felt strangely soft and welcoming. She wanted almost to bury herself in it, fall asleep and give up this crazy challenge. Yet how must her friends, tied up and imprisoned underground, be feeling? She was lucky – she had avoided capture.

Her task now was to rescue the others. They depended on her. She forced herself through the heather and onto the tufty grass higher up. One last push! She was nearly at the top and the slope was becoming gentler. She allowed herself a glance downwards. It made her shiver. Slippery black boulders sitting half out of the water glistened coldly far below, as if goading her to fall. The waves crashed angrily over the top of them.

Lou's stomach tightened at the sight and her head swam. That had been a mistake. She turned back to the slope and focused on what was ahead of her, rather than what lay below. On all fours, she scraped and scrabbled her way to the top of cliff, finally throwing herself over the edge and rolling forwards, away from the dangerous edge. She had made it! She found herself on a great stretch of fine, soft grass kept low by grazing sheep, several of which lay close by, fast asleep.

It was 10.45pm. It had taken half an hour to get to the top. In just fifteen minutes, Griffo and Mick's mates would arrive. Lou had to think quickly. Perhaps Griffo and Mick had gone off somewhere, planning to return at eleven for the rendezvous. If so, she might just have time to get to the others and set them free. It was a slim hope. Time was not on her side and most likely, Griffo and Mick would still be in the tunnel guarding their loot and making sure the others didn't try to escape.

I must get round there first, then decide what to do, Lou told herself, firmly. Her strength was recovering and her mind was sharpening. She got to her feet and stretched. What a relief to be able to stand up straight again! But there was no time to enjoy the moment. What was the best way?

Lou felt strangely disorientated. The mine entrance they had walked through earlier was more or less the other side of the hill but if she ploughed straight over the top, she would find herself up to her waist fighting through bracken and heather. If she could find the gully along which the brook ran, it would lead her more or less straight to it.

The mine workings overlooked the gully. Where were they? Lou ran along the grassy slope which headed downwards. That was promising. There was the rusting winding gear! It looked eerie in the moonlight but she was very relieved to see it. She was beginning to recover her sense of direction. As she approached, she heard the low gurgle of water. That must be the brook! She ran gratefully down to it.

She now needed to follow the path alongside it towards the mine entrance and the road beyond. This should not be a difficult task. She glanced at her watch: 10.50pm. She ignored her aching limbs and began to run as best she could. She slowed as she approached the mine entrance. Care was now more important than speed.

Nobody seemed to be about. She leapt off the path and onto the hillside where bracken and gorse would provide cover. Lou was more or less opposite the entrance now and could see and hear nothing save the babbling brook. A few yards on and she would be above the small parking area where visitors to Porth Ysgo left their cars.

'Blow!' muttered Lou, under her breath, when she saw Griffo and Mick's dirty white van. They must still be in the mine! That ended any hope of staging a rescue. In ten minutes' time their pals would be along to pick up millions of pounds worth of forged US dollars. As for Jack, David and Emily, what would happen to them? They might be spirited away and kidnapped by the gang, for all she knew. Lou simply had to stop these rogues escaping.

She took her rucksack off and hunted inside for her mobile phone. She was tired and getting flustered now. She couldn't even find the thing! The moon had gone again and she couldn't see what she was doing. Wherever was it? Ouch! Her sore, bruised fingers caught on something jagged. It was the rusty old knife from the mine. She cursed it, putting it in her pocket so it couldn't cut her again as she scrabbled about for the phone.

I remember now, thought Lou. It's in the small pouch, I put it in there so it would be easy to find. She got it out and pressed its buttons, willing its blue backlight to come on. It did so but flickered and then beeped with a warning that the battery needed charging. In any case, there was no signal. This was a very remote stretch of coast, of course. The phone was useless. There was no prospect of calling for help. She was on her own.

Lou strained to see her watch with the moon half behind a cloud. Just two minutes to go before the planned pick-up. She had done well to escape and get round to the mine entrance, but now what? She couldn't see how she could go underground to rescue her friends or stop the smugglers loading up their wagon and making off. She stared miserably at Griffo and Mick's van, nursing her cut finger. Ouch! That maddening antique knife was jabbing her thigh now through her pocket. She sat up and yanked it out, stupid thing.

Then she heard something in the distance. A rumbling, getting slowly louder. A shiver ran up and down her back and she clutched the blade protectively to her chest. She laughed at herself. What use could it be against a gang of smugglers armed with guns? Then it struck her. It might be useful. It just might be.

CHAPTER TWENTY-TWO

Desperate measures

WHILE Lou was struggling to find her way out of the manganese mine, Jack, David and Emily lay bound and gagged deep inside it. They had no idea what had happened to their friend, save for the fact that she wasn't with them. They felt scared without her but if she had evaded capture there was a glimmer of hope.

Griffo and Mick ignored the three youngsters. They walked back and forth to the passageway, piling up the sports bags, rucksacks and suitcases stuffed with fake banknotes, ready to be spirited away. Once the shelves had been stripped bare, the men used a couple of the bags as makeshift cushions and sat down on them.

'Right,' said Mick. 'We've got an hour before the others get here. I could do with a beer. Why don't we nip out, there's bound to be a pub round here. 'Those kids aren't going to go anywhere.'

'No way,' said Griffo. 'I'm a professional. I don't leave nuffin to chance. I've got a couple of cans in my rucksack, we'll drink them. Catch!' Griffo threw Mick a beer, then fished out packets of crisps. 'This'll keep us going.'

'Had we better give the kids something?' asked Mick, nervously.

'Naah,' said Griffo. 'I wasn't expectin' company. They'll have to go without.'

'What are we gonna do with them?' said Mick.

'Nuffin.' A nasty sneer crossed Griffo's face. 'The gaffer will go nuts if he knows those stupid kids have sussed what's been going on. It's too risky to let them free tonight.

'We'll leave 'em where they are and come back tomorrow and untie them. Or maybe the day after, or the day after that.'

Mick stared disbelievingly at Griffo, but the expression on his face was a warning it was not safe to start arguing. He swigged his beer and said nothing.

'Right,' said Griffo when the hour was nearly up. 'Five minutes to eleven, let's get moving.'

The men pushed their way past the baggage in the passageway, emerged from the mine and walked up the path through the kissing gate to the road.

'Should be here any minute now,' said Griffo, looking at his watch in the moonlight. The men heard a low rumble coming down the road and saw the flickering beam of headlights approaching.

Griffo's eyes and gold earring gleamed in anticipation in the pale light. He puffed out his ample chest and cleared his throat, rocking to and fro on the balls of his feet. He reckoned the gaffer would be well pleased with him. He would deliver millions of pounds of apparently perfect American dollars to him as promised and be richly rewarded for his efforts – not in fake money either, but bundles of genuine Bank of England tenners. As for Mick, he'd get what he deserved for all his blunders – a few crumbs from the master's table.

A battered old tourist coach which looked exactly like the sort used to take old folk on a day trip lumbered up the narrow lane and parked alongside Griffo and Mick's van. The rest of the gang had arrived.

Lou, watching from the shadowy hillside above, tingled with cold dread as the vehicle groaned up the lane and shuddered and jolted to a standstill. When she got a good look at their getaway vehicle, she stared in disbelief. It was almost comical.

Who would have thought that smugglers bringing in a huge quantity of forged currency would stash their loot inside a bumbling, decrepit holiday coach!

Exactly, who would have thought? That's the clever bit, she realised. No-one would suspect. And that's why they chose to use assorted suitcases, briefcases, rucksacks and sports bags. It could all be shoved out of sight into the luggage hold and if anyone looked inside, it would appear entirely innocent.

The driver's door creaked open and a burly figure alighted. Lou couldn't see the passenger side but thought she heard that door open, too. She could detect whispered voices but couldn't make out what was being said above the noisy tinkle of the brook. She strained to hear. Did she dare to get any nearer? She decided not to just yet. The scent of strong, foreign cigarettes rose in the night air.

Clang! That was the unmistakeable noise of the kissing gate banging shut. The men must have gone along the path to the mine. Lou sprang down the slope towards the parking area, taking care to keep in the shadows. She needed to see the coach from the front to be sure that no-one was about.

No-one was. Good! There was no time to lose. Lou darted up to the clapped-out coach, her heart thumping. She took another look around and listened intently. Satisfied that it was safe, she knelt alongside the front wheel on the passenger side, which was not visible from the kissing gate. Only the man in the moon could observe what she now did. In her clenched fist she held the rusty old miners' knife. She pressed its tip against the side of the coach tyre and pushed hard.

Just a little nick, a small injury to that tyre, was all she needed to inflict, enough to make it start deflating gently but not too fast. Lou knew that a puncture to the side wall of a tyre could not be repaired. The century-old knife was no longer sharp and the tyre was tough. Lou was forced to push at it hard, her sore hands crying out with pain. The tyre resisted stubbornly. Oh no, what was that? Torchlight, from the path beyond the kissing gate. Someone was coming!

Lou wrapped her fist around the knife and, in frustration and fury, pulled her arm back across her chest and stabbed with all her strength at the tyre. Propelled forwards by sheer anger, the knife finally penetrated the rubber. She wrenched the blade out and a slow 'psssss' of air escaped. She staggered to her feet and fled behind the coach as the torchlight flickered towards her, nearly catching her.

One tyre was not enough, they would have a spare – she needed to puncture a rear tyre as well. The men were now at the side of the coach. She heard a key turn in the lock and the grumbling squeal of a stiff door being pulled open. That would be the luggage compartment, no doubt, ready to be filled with an illicit cargo.

Lou yearned to flee into the safety of the dark hillside, but that wasn't an option. Instead, she cowered behind the rear wheel on the driver's side. She jabbed at it but the knife blade bounced off.

No good! She had to be furious like she was before and make that fury power the knife forwards.

She looked at the tyre, imagining it was a smuggler's ugly round chest and stabbed again as hard as she could. That wasn't a nice thing to think but it did the trick. Hissssss – went the air as it escaped through the gash.

Lou bounded back onto the hillside, diving behind a bush, then crawling on all fours to a safe distance. That second tyre had taken a good slash and she knew it. The air would ebb from it rapidly. The coach wouldn't be able to get very far down the road now, thanks to her.

From her vantage point on the hillside, Lou allowed herself a few moments' satisfaction as she looked down on the sabotaged vehicle alongside Griffo and Mick's white van.

The van! Lou groaned in dismay. What about *its* tyres?

Keep calm, she told herself, she must not lose her nerve. The four men were going in convoy to and fro to the mine, no-one would see her if she sneaked back and gave them a nip as well. She slithered back down the slope and over to the parking area.

She attacked the rear passenger tyre first. The knife cut through the rubber fairly cleanly – van tyres were clearly not as tough as those fitted to a heavy coach. She scurried round to the front and crouched by the wheel on the driver's side.

As she lifted the blade ready to strike, she noticed a light flashing towards the van. Two men were approaching! Blow, had they finished loading already? Lou did not have time to run clear. She lay flat and rolled herself beneath the van, a heavy boot missing her fingers by a fraction of a second. A key turned in the lock, someone was getting in, then someone else got in the other side. Griffo and Mick, presumably.

The van bounced up and down above her as the hefty pair took their seats. Despite her fright and the extreme danger she was in, Lou stabbed into the inner side of the tyre. It punctured instantly and began to hiss. The headlights went on and the engine roared. The wheel Lou had attacked swivelled. It was about to reverse towards her.

She rolled out of its path and into the ditch just in time. They could see her through the side windows if they looked carefully. But it was dark and her clothes were blackened and dirty from the crawl through the mine. They would blend in well with the mud she was now lying in. The van's gearbox clanked and clunked as Griffo prepared to drive away.

'Please, please don't see me,' Lou whispered.

The van hovered motionless in the middle of the road with its engine running. Why the delay? They must have spotted her! At any moment, Lou expected to hear a car door open and feel Griffo's coarse hands on her shoulders. She screwed her eyes tightly shut and waited to be grabbed.

It didn't happen. The coach juddered into reverse, expelling a choking cloud of exhaust fumes. Griffo and Mick were simply hanging back while their pals pulled out and drove off. They followed behind in convoy. Eventually, her ears brought her the good news. The raucous din from two badly-maintained diesel engines slowly faded into the distance. She opened her eyes a fraction. The parking area was empty. The smugglers had gone!

Lou sprang up instantly and slipped silently through the kissing gate, taking care not to let it clang shut. They just might have left someone on guard. Knife still in her hand, she slipped towards the mine entrance. It was difficult to see in the darkness, but the men had made it easier, trampling a clear path through the bracken right to it.

She resisted the temptation to dash straight in and paused for a moment listening intently. The brook babbled; a far-off sheep baa-ed; the sea thundered ashore; but that was all.

Lou walked slowly, carefully, into the mine. Total silence. She could not, of course, see a thing. But she would hear sure enough if the others cried for help. A cold dread swept over her. Had the men taken them? She didn't think so but she couldn't be certain.

She groped her way along the passage towards the cavern where they had found the smugglers' hidey-hole. A light glimmered inside. Lou tiptoed in the shadows. A torch lay in the middle of the floor emitting a weak glow. The shelves which once heaved with baggage were now stripped bare. A couple of squashed beer cans lay on the floor and what was that? It looked like a piece of half-eaten pizza similar to the one Lou had seen in Mick's hotel bedroom.

There was no way to be absolutely sure that no smuggler remained behind but Lou needed to find the others quickly. The smugglers could not, after all, get clean away thanks to her work on their tyres. She snapped her torch on and pointed it in all directions.

And there were Jack, David and Emily, thank goodness! Still tied up and gagged and shoved at the back of the cavern. She bounded over and at first they recoiled in fright at this strange, dirty figure with a knife, not realising at first who it was.

'It's me, Lou, now do you want rescuing or not?' she whispered to them.

She cut Emily free first, struggling to pierce the coarse cloth she had been trussed up with. She gave the frightened girl a hug and then released the others. In the dim light, their dirt-streaked faces broke into weak smiles. Lou had come back and rescued them! One after another they hugged her tight and thanked her profusely.

'Come on, we are still in danger, we must get out and fast,' said Lou. 'Get your rucksacks and let's go. As soon as we're out of here, Jack, we'll try and use your mobile phone to call for help. It probably won't work but it's worth a go.'

'It definitely won't, the men took the battery out,' said Jack.

'They left you here to rot as well, the scum,' replied Lou, grimly, wishing she'd slashed every one of their tyres. 'Come on, let's get out of here.'

The others followed her in single file out of the mine and onto the path. They wanted to hug her again but she pushed them away.

'There's no time for that,' she hissed, impatiently. 'The smugglers have gone but they won't get far. I've cut their tyres. I couldn't let them get away in case they had you with them. They may well head back when they realise what has happened and we have no way of calling the police.'

'We cycled past a farmhouse earlier just up the road from here,' said Jack. 'Would we have time to nip along to it?' Despite his tiredness, he was determined to do his bit.

'No,' replied Lou. 'It's too risky. We might well walk straight into them. We can't go the other way either, in case they send for help and it comes from that direction. We must stay off the road.'

Lou paused. She was not normally indecisive but she was desperately tired and keen not to make any mistakes. She badly wanted this day to end now. In the moonlight, the others could see the weariness and worry etched into her face beneath the grime.

'We must go where they'll least expect,' she said. 'When they find out you've gone they'll search the roads first, then the hillside. They'll comb it with powerful torches and may even bring dogs here to track our scent. I wouldn't put anything past them. Our best bet is to head to the beach – we can hide behind the big rocks on the shore and dogs won't be able to track us through sea water.'

She swung the torch in front of her, guiding the way as the moon again disappeared under a cloud. 'There are steep, wooden steps to the beach. Be careful not to trip and fall.'

One after the other, the children slowly lowered their aching limbs down the steps, clinging hard to the rail as they went. At the bottom they stepped out onto the shingle of the small, rock-bound Porth Ysgo beach.

'Fantastic, there is a boat moored in the bay,' exclaimed Lou, shining her torch towards it. 'That's a piece of good luck which I wasn't expecting. There must be fishermen around. The tide is on the turn, they must have come to fish the tide in. Shoals of fish often come closer into shore at night. This is good news, we must see if we can find them.'

Emily glanced nervously up at the hillside. 'Oh Lou, look!,' she cried. 'There's a light up there behind us.' Lou swung round in dismay.

A cold, hard voice rang out: 'They're down here, let's get them!'

They were trapped!

'Follow me into the water!' ordered Lou.

She handed Jack the torch and began to wade out to the fishing boat as swiftly as she could. It wasn't all that far out but with her energy levels so low, it was a tough battle. Jack passed the torch to David and plunged after her, fearing for her safety.

He wasn't sure quite what Lou intended, but knew that she was dangerously tired. The water came up to their shoulders and they were forced to swim the final few yards. David remained with Emily who was not strong enough to make it to the boat.

Panting, Lou and Jack pulled themselves on board. Lou began hauling up the anchor. Her cut and bruised hands struggled with the weight but Jack tugged as well and between them they wrenched it up. Lou turned to the engine, patting its sides with her hands for the starting cord.

'I've got it!' she cried. Lou tried to give it a good yank but there was just no power left in her arms. Jack took over and pulled hard while she grabbed the tiller. The engine roared and the boat leapt forwards. Lou brought its nose round, pointing towards the shore.

The smugglers' boots thudded speedily down the wooden steps. David and Emily were up to their knees in water; in desperation they waded out further, until they were up to their chests.

'Come here, you vandals,' shouted an angry voice, 'you're coming with us. How did you escape!'

Pebbles scrunched under the smugglers' feet as they ran towards the shore.

'Help Lou, help!' cried Emily.

There was not time to haul David and Emily aboard before the men pounced on them and Lou knew it. The men would leap aboard themselves. That would be a disaster.

Lou pushed the tiller hard over, span the boat around and headed out to sea. Jack looked at her baffled. So did the others. What *was* she doing?

CHAPTER TWENTY-THREE

Moonlit drama

LOU swivelled the boat round again, its bow pointing directly at the men as they began to wade into the water. She throttled up the engine. With an almighty roar, the boat surged forwards, bouncing through the waves, sending up great plumes of spray.

The two men were seconds away from grabbing David and Emily, but they halted, their hard eyes fixed on the fishing boat now powering straight towards them.

As it approached, they staggered back, eyes wide in horror. The boat was going to hit them! But with a split second to spare, Lou swerved, sending a wall of foaming water crashing over their heads, knocking them off their feet and submerging them.

Lou allowed a smirk of satisfaction to cross her weary face. She pulled up alongside David and Emily and cut the engine. She grabbed Emily, and Jack got hold of David as the pair stretched out their arms. They heaved them on board and all four collapsed in a heap on the floor of the boat.

Jack and Lou leapt up instantly. They would only have a few seconds before the smugglers righted themselves and were after them again. Jack, knowing his extra strength was required, tugged the starter cord as Lou took the tiller. The boat rapidly surged into the middle of the bay, safely out of harm's way.

'Help me with the anchor, Jack,' said Lou. The pair of them threw the heavy steel hook back overboard. 'Now, a good, modern fishing boat like this should have a ship-to-shore radio,' she added. 'It's time to get the police to round these people up and stick them where they belong.'

The others nodded, their worried faces pale and serious.

Lou shone her torch at the dashboard. 'Excellent. I've found it. Ok, I think I remember how to do this. We'll soon find out!'

She switched on the radio and to her relief, the display illuminated with the number 16. That meant 'channel 16' – the emergency channel, which was the one she needed. It occurred to her that she didn't actually know the boat's name. She peered over the side. It was called Sara Anne.

She unhooked the radio microphone, pressed the transmit button and spoke softly, not wishing to be overheard from the shore: 'MAYDAY MAYDAY. This is the Sara Anne. We are located in the bay at Porth Ysgo. We require urgent assistance, over.'

A man's voice crackled back over the airwaves. 'Sara Anne, this is Holyhead coastguard, state what assistance you require, over.

'Holyhead Coastguard, this is Sara Anne. We wish to report that a smuggling gang is on the shore at Porth Ysgo. They are using the old mines at Nant Gadwen on the hillside overlooking the beach to store illegal goods. They took my friends prisoner but I managed to rescue them. We are just a group of children, we ran into the sea and jumped on board this fishing boat. We have anchored in the bay, over.'

There was what seemed to be a slight pause before the crisp voice of the coastguard replied: 'Sara Anne, this is Holyhead coastguard. Message received and will be relayed to North Wales Police. Please stand by on this channel.'

'I bet it's not every day the coastguard gets a distress call like that. I hope he believed me!' Lou smiled cheerfully at the others; she still looked dishevelled, but her weariness seemed to have left her. Her high spirits gave the others new-found strength.

Meanwhile, something of a commotion was underway ashore. The two soaking wet smugglers had been joined by two of their mates. Then a couple of fishermen turned up and demanded to know what was going on. But the smugglers, steaming with rage, were in no mood to offer any explanations.

The smugglers shouted themselves hoarse at the children, now anchored infuriatingly out of reach. At the same time, the fishermen were shouting angrily at the smugglers.

'Come back here!' bawled what sounded like Mick at the children.

'Come and get us!' yelled Lou.

'What on earth is going on,' demanded one of the fishermen. 'Give us our boat back at once!'

'We haven't got your blasted boat,' snarled another smuggler, who sounded like Griffo. 'Those kids are nothing to do with us!'

'Why are you chasing them then, there's something suspicious going on if you ask me,' replied the fisherman.

'I think we better phone the police,' said the other fisherman, reaching inside his rucksack.

'You'll do no such thing,' said Griffo. 'It's just a misunderstanding that's all. We'll help you get your boat back, don't worry.'

The squabbling men failed to notice another boat chugging into the bay. Suddenly a powerful searchlight shone from it onto them all and from its cabin roof, a blue light began to flash on and off.

'It's the police,' cried Lou. 'They've got here. That was quick!'

Another strong beam shone down, making the men on the beach blink. This time, it was from the cliff-top above. Footsteps could be heard coming down the wooden steps. Then a clear, stern voice rang out: 'Police! You're under arrest.'

Suddenly, about a dozen police officers appeared from the shadows. They pounced on the men and pulled their arms behind their backs.

'Wait,' shouted Lou from the boat. 'Two of them are innocent fishermen. The other four are the smugglers.'

It was easy enough to see who was who, since the fishermen were holding rods. The police let them go. Griffo, Mick and their two accomplices whose names the children didn't know were escorted away, stumbling back across the shingle with their hands cuffed to officers, cursing and snarling as they went and shouting nasty threats to the children.

The police boat pulled up alongside the *Sara Anne* and an officer helped the children climb aboard. Rugs were thrown around them to keep them warm and hot drinks handed up from the galley. Lou was anxious to tell them about the old-fashioned tourist coach the smugglers had used as a get-away vehicle.

'Oh they were using that ramshackle old thing? And a scruffy little van? We passed them on the way, abandoned at the side of the road.'

'Those vehicles both belong to the smugglers. You'll find the luggage compartment of the coach full of baggage containing bundles of fake superdollars, worth millions of pounds,' said Lou.

As the police boat sped away from Porth Ysgo towards Aberdaron, she began to tell the full story of their brush with the smugglers – beginning with David's overheard conversation on the beach at Abersoch. Lou took them through the find of the mystery case on St Tudwal's Island; the raid on Mick's hotel bedroom; the photographed diary entries leading them to Whistling Sands; their boat coming in at night; how Jack had filmed them . . .'

The police officers listened, enthralled, but Lou's voice slurred and trailed off. The gentle up-and-down rhythm of the boat in the water and the chug chug of the engine had lulled her to sleep. She lolled forward and Jack put out his arms to steady her. He gazed affectionately at her exhausted, dirt-streaked face. Louise Elliott had not only saved them from the clutches of a major criminal gang, she had effectively smashed it.

'You can all be proud of yourselves,' said the officer to him. 'With these men in custody and the evidence you have gathered, they will go to prison for a long time. We'll be recommending you for an award!'

With those words of praise ringing in his ears, Jack too fell asleep where he sat. As for Emily and David, they had closed their eyes long before. The children didn't hear the boat arrive in Aberdaron, and barely noticed as they were placed gently into the back of a waiting car and whisked along dark country lanes back to Abersoch.

The day after, they would need to tell their astonished parents what had happened, make full statements to the police and hand over the photographs and videos which would be crucial evidence for when the smugglers were brought before a judge. But right then, their only task was to collapse into soft, cosy beds and sleep and, no doubt, to dream some very strange dreams.

CHAPTER TWENTY-FOUR

Some news on Lou's cottage

THE following day the youngsters did not see anything of Lou. Mr and Mrs Johnson wanted to keep a close eye on them and anyway, they all had to be interviewed by the police which took quite some time.

Lou sent Jack a text message asking him to meet her at 11am on Tuesday, the day after, on the rocks beneath the path to her parents' holiday cottage. Jack set off after a hearty caravan breakfast and no petty squabbles with his brother this time. They seemed to get on better these days.

He strolled through the dunes and down onto the beach. The enchantment he felt as he beheld the open sea swept across him once again, just as it had on the first day of their holiday.

So much had happened since, he almost expected the view to have changed. It hadn't, of course. The sea sparkled cheerfully and the lighthouse on the smaller island gleamed white. When he had last looked upon it from this spot, he had no idea that within days he would end up sailing there and picnicking on the grass in front of it with a wild, headstrong girl called Louise Elliott. It was hard to believe they had known her for barely a week. It seemed like she had been their friend for ages.

Jack leapt onto the rocks beneath her holiday cottage, looking up at the stone steps which led to it. He was a few minutes early but that was fine, it was a moment to savour. He was aching to talk over their amazing adventure with her. Then a sad thought crossed his mind. The cottage was due to be sold that very day! Amid the excitement he had forgotten.

Jack sat on the bottom step, gazing at the boats bobbing

about in the harbour. The view no longer seemed quite so magical. He doubted it ever would again. Once Lou's holiday home had been sold they would be unlikely to see her again. A tear ran down his cheek. He lifted a hand to wipe it away.

Another hand got there first. He had not noticed a striking-looking girl with long black hair and emerald eyes slipping down the steps behind him.

'It's ok, Jack,' said Lou, softly, reading his thoughts as she sat alongside him. 'I know why you're sad – but there's no need. Dad's just done a deal to sell the most amazing story to newspapers and magazines around the world, and he thinks there may even be a book in it. It will bring in thousands of pounds – which means we can keep the cottage, for a good long while anyway.'

'What story has your dad got?' replied Jack, struggling to take it all in. 'I thought he didn't have much work on?'

'You are dopey at times, aren't you,' chided Lou. '*Our* story of course! The real-life account of how a bunch of kids smashed a major smuggling ring. Dad was so proud of me – well, all of us. He thinks we're brilliant.'

Jack looked at her in delight. 'That's fantastic,' he spluttered, scarcely able to believe it.

'The police told me yesterday they had been after this gang for ages and it's thanks to us they have finally nabbed them,' continued Lou. 'They just could not believe it when they found all those bundles of fake dollars in the bags and cases. The men had taken the baggage out of the coach and hidden everything behind the hedge before they came storming after us.

'It didn't take the police long to find it all though. The cash was on its way to the Midlands to fund major organised crime and drug dealing – just as we thought. The police knew the gang had stopped using the port at Holyhead, but had no idea how they were getting their loot across – until we solved the mystery for them! Griffo,

Mick and their mates will be locked up for a long time, so we're all safe at Abersoch now. We can meet up in the future and have plenty more fun together.'

Jack felt overwhelmed by this detailed account. When he tried to reply, the words somehow got stuck in his throat. The emotion of the last couple of days had caught up with him.

Lou gave his arm a squeeze. 'It's great news, isn't it? I wanted you to be the first to know, as you and I became friends first out of the four of us.'

'I really am sorry for trespassing that day, though,' joked Jack.

'I'm so glad you did, or I'd never have met you all,' said Lou, grinning. 'Come on, let's go for a stroll along the beach together and talk about smugglers and hidden money and long-forgotten mines. Then we'll find the others and take them out in the boat for a picnic. But if we come across any more smugglers today, do you know what we're going to do?'

He shook his head.

'We're going to look the other way and ignore them,' said Lou. 'I just want to relax for now.'

'That sounds like a very good plan,' said Jack.

LOU ELLIOTT MYSTERY ADVENTURES:

1. Smugglers at Whistling Sands
2. The Missing Treasure
3. Something Strange in the Cellar
4. Trouble at Chumley Towers

George Chedzoy works from home as a novelist and freelance writer. He lives in North Wales with his wife and two young children. He's always pleased to hear from readers and you can contact him directly on email or Twitter (see below). All books in this series can be ordered from bookshops or from Amazon.

George's blog: http://georgechedzoy.blogspot.com
Twitter: @georgechedzoy
Email: georgechedzoy@hotmail.co.uk